Mouse

The Superhero School series

By
Donna Sager Cowan
Illustrated by Diane J. Reid

Text copyright © 2018 by Donna Sager Cowan

Illustrations copyright © 2018 by Diane J. Reid

Printed in the United States of America

Published by:

Author Academy Elite

P.O. Box 43

Powell, OH 43035

Paperback ISBN-13: 978-1-64085-382-9

Hardcover ISBN-13: 978-1-64085-383-6

Library of Congress Control Number: 2018952844

Chapter One

A GREAT SHADOW fell across the field, yet the mouse didn't run. He shook one fist and hurled a pebble at the diving hawk.

"Come on, you mean old hawk! Just try to have me for breakfast!" He flung the words toward the sky.

The hawk hardly noticed the small stone when it bumped against his chest before hitting the ground. Curious behavior for a mouse. The hawk cocked his head to stare one-eyed at his prey. This mouse would be a tasty snack before the next hunt.

The hawk stretched his sharp claws and swooped down to the field, wingtips skimming the grass. He snatched the mouse with a quick plunge and pluck. His wings gained air with each mighty flap.

"So you think you've won? Well, I have a surprise for you!" the mouse yelled, wiggling his arms loose from the hawk's talons. He dug through his pockets and pulled out a pair of golden nail clippers. Brow furrowed, the mouse focused on every clip and snip.

After the third claw fell away, the hawk looked down to see what the mouse was doing. He watched in horror as his beautiful, sharp talons disappeared, each one trimmed to a nub. The hawk gaped, helpless, as the mouse slipped from his grasp and fell.

The hawk worried that he wouldn't be able to catch anything with claws that now resembled neatly trimmed fingernails. Embarrassed to have been outwitted by a mouse, the hawk flew to a nearby tree to hide.

● ● ●

Simon Cheddar prided himself on being prepared. That's why he wore a vest and overcoat. Their many pockets, nooks, and folds, kept his tools and treasures tucked away. Today would have been much worse, if not for those clippers he'd stashed away for later.

He never knew what would prove useful. His vest and coat linings held an abundance of found items. String. A needle. A thimble. Matches. A bottle cap. Rubber bands. Thumbtacks. And a cotton ball. Lots more, but he only remembered the things he saw while searching for the clippers.

Now, falling through the air, he had an even bigger problem—one he wasn't sure anything in his pockets would solve. Simon gulped as he looked down into the hungry gold-green eyes of a gray and white cat.

Simon panicked. He was falling fast. He didn't have wings, nor did he know any birds to call for help. He was going to die. Escaping that hawk hadn't saved him after all.

Simon sorted through his pockets for a solution. He considered each item before tossing it aside.

Maybe use some string to turn his overcoat into a makeshift parachute?

No.

Not enough time.

If he wrapped himself inside the cotton ball, he could bounce softly instead of smacking the hard, rocky ground.

Nope. Wouldn't work.

The cotton ball wasn't big enough.

Simon watched the cat pace in a large circle. It looked up and down, between Simon and the ground, trying to find the best spot to catch him.

• • •

All the joy Simon had felt melted away. He was prepared to die from the fall. That was an honorable death. Simon wouldn't mind that.

But being eaten by a cat? Not without a fight, Simon thought.

His body fell faster. The distance between him and the waiting cat grew smaller. The cat loomed, its teeth gleaming in the sunshine.

Simon considered the items left in his pockets. He pulled each one out, dismissed it, and let it fall away. Then the tip of his nail caught on a small stick of wood, hidden along the seam. His tiny paw clutched the matchstick, while a brilliant plan took form.

Timing was everything.

• • •

Simon held his breath. He was so close to the cat, he swore he could feel its breath as it hissed past those menacing teeth.

Simon counted slowly. He held the matchstick like a battle sword, then struck it across his worn sleeve. Simon watched the small flame sputter to life, praying the wind wouldn't blow it out. He closed his eyes, swallowed hard, and hoped the universe was on his side.

This plan would either be his greatest…or his last.

When Simon felt the cat's whiskers tickle his toes, he opened his eyes and aimed for its gaping mouth. He jammed the lit match between the cat's fangs, then, using the stick like a monkey bar, swung himself down to the ground.

Simon shook the dirt from his rumpled vest and coat. He gathered his scattered treasures, stuffing them back inside his pockets.

Chapter Two

"OUCH!" CATT HISSED, spitting out the match and patting her burnt whisker. "Why'd ya do that?" She squinted down at the mouse, trying to hold back tears.

"Just trying to survive until dinnertime." Simon clamped a paw over his runaway mouth. He shouldn't talk about food, especially when he was on the menu!

Stupid, stupid, stupid! Come on, Simon, he thought to himself. You're smarter than this. Now think.

A sly smile spread across his face. "I have some ointment for that," he said, "if you promise to not eat me."

● ● ●

"Ointment?" Catt stopped fussing with her whisker. "Why would I eat you?" she asked.

A furrow crept over Catt's brow as she considered the strange mouse. "I, uh, mean—I mean…really?"

She heard the uncertainty in her voice. Catt pulled herself up tall, locked her jaw, and forced her loudest, hardest voice. "I could promise and still eat you."

Catt couldn't believe she actually said that. Now she sounded dumb and mean. Great.

"What a worthless cat."

No matter how many times her owners said it, she didn't believe them.

She wasn't worthless.

She deserved a life, with friends and maybe even a family.

She was better than a punchline for their jokes.

Even without a real name.

She wasn't worthless.

● ● ●

Simon watched the cat's eyes scrunch, then widen. Her nose twitched, her cheeks puffed and hollowed with every thought that chased across her mind. He knew that look. He'd seen it many times. Fear. This cat was afraid, and she was desperate not to show how much. What would scare a cat? he wondered.

Simon chuckled as he brushed a spot of dirt from his coat. He sifted through his pockets, checking that all his treasures were inside.

"Yes," he said, "I know. Cats are tricksters. But you did sort of save me. I would have died from the fall if it hadn't been for you." Peering from under thick lashes, Simon waited, ready to duck from a quick swipe.

"Best to soothe their ego, boy. Cats can be moody beasts!" Simon could hear the words as clear as the first time Grandma Whisker said them, shaking a bony finger on one paw, with the other resting on her wide hip.

Grandma's cat lectures were legendary. Having lost her husband, as well as Simon's mother and sister, to cats, she knew a thing or two about feline danger, and she made sure Simon learned too. He recalled her every caution since the day he went to live with Grandma Whisker.

Simon was willing to help anyone, but he wouldn't ever trust a cat.

● ● ●

Catt considered the mouse's offer carefully. She pointed one sharp claw at his coat pocket. "You really have ointment in there?"

"Sure do." Simon puffed out his chest, tucked his thumbs into his coat lapels, and pushed up onto his toes. "Found it last week, so it's as good as new."

"Let's see it," Catt demanded, craning her neck to see inside his pockets.

Simon stepped back, shaking one finger under Catt's nose. "Nope," he said. "You gotta swear an oath first."

"An oath? What's that?" she asked, cocking her head.

"It's a big promise," Simon said, walking heel-to-toe in front of the riveted Catt. "And you can't break it. No matter what. It's the most important promise you'll make."

"What if I break my promise? Who's gonna care?" Catt sneered, licking her sore whisker before pulling her lips into an evil smile.

Simon stepped under the cat's long, bright teeth.

He whispered, "You'll know."

"So?" Catt hissed, rolling her eyes. "Doesn't mean anything. I can still do what I want." She nudged Simon with each word. "And-you-can't-do-anything-about-it!"

Simon sighed and shook his head. "You're right. I can't do anything about all those days and nights you'll suffer. All those regrets, about how it could have been different. How you could have been GREAT!" He swiped at an imaginary tear. "If only you could see past right now—to see how hollow your life will be, all because you broke a promise."

Simon looked up at Catt. "I'm just a mouse, but I'm prepared to die. I've lived a full life with lots of adventures. But

9

I worry about you. A cat who is too afraid to keep a promise, too afraid to do the right thing. It's sad."

Simon turned around, then looked back over his shoulder. "I feel sorry for you, cat."

Sighing, he shifted through his pockets, removing objects and laying them on the ground in two neat piles.

"I guess the teacher from Superhero School was right," he said. "Choices make heroes, not powers."

Simon removed his prized overcoat and vest, folded them, and placed them on top of the piles.

"Okay. I'm ready." Simon gulped. "Just make it quick. I'm not much for torture."

Simon knelt, trembling in front of the cat's claws. He stretched out his neck and waited for the final blow.

Chapter Three

"SUPERHERO SCHOOL?" CATT yanked the mouse up so they were nose to nose. "What's that? Can anyone go? Can you get me in?"

She squished Simon's face, closer with each sputtered question. Simon couldn't answer, since his mouth was pushed against her upper lip. A bead of sweat rolled down his cheek. When Catt realized how tight she was holding him, she set him back on his feet and took a big step backward.

Simon shuddered. His heart raced. He sucked in a deep breath, set to hurtle to the nearest hole, when he looked again at the cat. Her mouth frowned, her eye whiskers arched. She looked curious, not threatening. She wasn't trying to scare him. This cat wanted to know about the school.

A soft chuckle escaped when Simon released the breath he'd been holding. He collected his leftover treasures, stuffing them haphazardly into his pockets. To most, his pockets looked like a jumbled mess. But Simon had a system: left coat pocket for weapons; right coat pocket for repairs and new ideas; right vest pocket for anything shiny; and left vest pocket for the rest.

Meanwhile, an animated Catt prattled on, having forgotten her singed whisker. "…animals shouldn't intermix… cats are smarter…might lower my standards to be seen with a mouse…"

He could kick himself for mentioning the school. But dealing with a cat was stressful, and he'd already had a hectic morning. Almost headlining the breakfast menu twice should excuse any lapse in judgement.

● ● ●

"Okay, okay!" Simon pressed his paws down in a calming motion. "You want to go to Superhero School, right?"

He cocked his head, searching for any sign that she was about to grab him again.

"No, I want to be a superhero!" she said, every muscle tensed, every hair stood on end.

Simon stepped back, inclined to run. But then she plopped down, as if all the air left her body.

"Okay, okay," he soothed. "But you have to go to Superhero School before you can be a superhero."

Catt dropped her chin to her chest. She circled one claw in the dirt. "What is Superhero School? Is that for apprentices?"

"Apprentices?"

"Yeah. You know…fetching, carrying, cleaning…for a real superhero?"

When Catt looked to see Simon's reaction, he was pacing.

"No, it's not like that," he said. "It's training. It's a school where you learn—"

"I can learn!" Catt interrupted.

"—to be super," Simon finished.

"I can be super," she said with less enthusiasm.

"Well…" He rubbed the back of his damp neck. "It's not exactly a school. It's complicated."

"Oh, how?" One cat ear swiveled toward Simon. A feeling of doom tingled across Catt's skin. She expected him to change his mind or tell her she wasn't welcome.

Simon ran a finger along his too-tight collar. He prayed for an interruption so he could run away. "It's not an actual school school. It's a class…at the Community Center…"

"Hmmm. Tell me more." Catt's lips stretched into a strange grin as she buffed her nails against her chest.

• • •

Simon swallowed around a huge lump in his throat.

He was a great talker. He could talk legs off a chair, as Grandma Whisker would say. Think, Simon, think!

How could he explain the greatest thing ever and not sound insane? Superhero School was the reason he'd left the safety of Mouseville and risked his life. He'd do almost anything to attend today's first class.

Mouseville needed a superhero, and Simon intended to be it. Then, instead of hiding from predators, the citizens of Mouseville could thrive in society.

No one thinks about what life is like for a mouse. Mice are small and pesky. Their every move is planned for escape or survival. Simon hated it. He wanted to go on a simple walk across the field to town, without fear.

Simon's destiny was Superhero School.

Even if he had to drag a crazy, gullible cat along to get there.

Simon squared his shoulders, drew himself up to his full three inches, and stepped right under Catt's nose.

"Look—"He coughed once. "It's a school. It teaches us stuff we need to know, with plenty of challenges. This isn't a game, and I'm going. Come with me, or don't. But we leave now."

Simon offered his paw. "I'm Simon Cheddar. You coming or what?"

=^.,.^=

Chapter Four

CATT EYED SIMON Cheddar to see if he was tricking her. Finally, she raised her paw, enclosing Simon's smaller one, and said, "Catt, with two tees. And I promise I won't eat you."

Their paws pumped once, quick, and dropped to their sides. Both Simon and Catt took a big step back.

Simon scanned the tree line and prayed that no one saw them acting like friends. Then he dug in his pocket and tossed a tube of ointment to the cat.

"Catt? That's kind of an odd name, isn't it?" Simon tried not to smile as she rubbed medicine on her whisker.

"Yeah, yeah, yeah. Laugh all you want." Catt rolled her eyes. "I've been teased a lot about my name."

She thought Simon seemed nice. Maybe he would understand.

"The people who owned me didn't give me a name. They called me cat. Like, 'that cat needs food,' 'that cat wants out,' 'that cat stinks.' So, when they dumped me in the alley, I decided to make my own rules. I added a second tee and gave myself a new name."

"You lived with humans?" Simon bellowed. He looked around, as though expecting a human to jump out from behind a blade of grass. "Where?"

"It's this place called California."

"Cali-what? I've never heard of it." Simon didn't like the sound of a place where humans owned animals.

Simon and Catt traded stories about life in Sweet Meadows compared to California. Simon told Catt all about Mouseville and Grandma Whisker and his cousin Joe. He spoke of Sweet Meadows and a yellow house and an old lady cat named Mrs. Gee.

According to Catt, animals didn't talk in California. They didn't have homes or jobs. They were either pets or pests. Simon wasn't sure what the difference was, but both sounded awful. He never wanted to live in a place like that.

"Do you want a different name?" Simon asked. " 'Cause we could give you a new one."

Catt scratched her chin. "Naw. I think I'll keep it. Someday I might change it, but I'm good for now."

"You're sure?"

Catt nodded, then they turned to walk toward the Sweet Meadows town and Superhero School.

● ● ●

Simon and Catt traveled in silence, both lost inside their own thoughts. Catt tried to imagine what attending school was like. Simon worried about sneaking Catt into class. Sign-ups began weeks ago and, last he checked, the class was full.

When they arrived at the Community Center, Simon touched Catt's leg. "It's in Room 207."

They hurried up the wide steps, through the front doors and crowded hallway, and finally into Room 207.

Simon and Catt grabbed two desks near the front. Once her heart stopped racing, Catt looked around. She found a surprising mix of animals.

At the back, a black and white pig tried to hide her ample frame behind a small desk. Her flesh flowed over the seat and pushed through the slats. Her broad chest and plump belly squeezed so tight between the desk and seat that the joints groaned. Screws squeaked with every nervous shift.

The pig wore a purple hooded cape. The material floated, soft, like curling smoke, around her body. The cape was exquisite and seemed too bold for such a shy pig. Beneath the hood, her eyes pointed down at the desktop.

Catt knew that look. That pig wished she were invisible. Perhaps she thought the cape would hide her. But it didn't work. Catt knew from experience that when you try to blend in, the more you stand out.

Catt tapped Simon on the shoulder and pointed to an owl sitting two rows behind and on the left. The peculiar bird studied every occupant of the room with slow, blinking eyes. He watched each new student arrive with the same diligent study, and, after each observation, he scribbled on a notepad.

Catt's thoughts scattered when two dogs entered. One was a schnauzer (the same as the neighbor's dog that always barked at her), and the other a teacup poodle. They debated dog treats in loud, shrill voices.

A well-shorn lamb, in an orange paisley designer dress, strutted in like she was on a Paris runway. She scanned the room, decided they were all unimportant, and flounced to an open desk, clutching her phone like a life preserver.

Behind her, twin Siamese cats leered. When they came upon the dogs, they hissed and growled and flicked their tails up. After sneering at Catt, the twins halted mid-step when they saw Simon. Licking their lips, their eyes traveled over his body, dividing him up for a snack.

Simon's uneasy gaze followed the cats as they moved across the room. He prepared himself for a sudden dash under the desk.

• • •

Catt hated them for making Simon nervous. They were bullies, through and through. But picking on the smaller and weaker was lazy. Those two would never last in a fair fight. Catt wished she could give them a taste of what it felt like to be bullied. That might change their minds. But probably not. Mean was mean, and it didn't often change.

Catt noticed the hair on her tail standing up. She hated being bushy. She stroked her fur down, while entertaining thoughts of justice for bullies.

Simon and Catt startled when a goat asked if this was the superhero class. It had slipped in without even the owl's notice, considering his surprised stare.

A brown cow leaned between two crammed bookcases. His leather jacket hung open, a small tattoo peeking out.

A tree frog hopped by, taking the seat beside the pig. A llama marched to the closest unoccupied desk, slumped in the seat, and fell asleep. His soft snores sang in the nervous quiet.

• • •

Surely another rodent type would attend the class, Simon thought. Maybe a squirrel or a gopher or a rat. But not one came. Paws clenching the edge of his desk, Simon counted the remaining seats. He couldn't be the only mouse. Mice could be superheroes too. Right? His neck itched. He stuck his paws under his legs and willed them to stop shaking.

A chicken waddled in with a grain sack, tossing wing-fulls of seeds into her open beak. Two birds, a blue jay and a robin, flew through the door and circled the room twice before landing.

A brown pony and a white rabbit slid into the last two empty seats just as the bell rang.

The classroom door closed with an ominous click.

• • •

Wait, where was their teacher?

How did the door close by itself?

Catt and Simon looked around in shock. Students stared open-mouthed at the door.

Then the lights dimmed.

A projection screen lowered from the ceiling but remained dark.

Catt's head whipped from the door to the screen to the other students and back again. With so many strange things vying for her attention, she felt dizzy. She needed to lie down.

Finally, a cool, precise voice filled the room.

"Welcome to Superhero School."

=^.,.^=

Chapter Five

MURMURS AND RESTLESS fidgeting ensued.

The voice began again, silencing the students. "I know everyone has questions. What does it take to be a superhero? When do we get to the cool stuff? Let's start with some answers. First, everyone will learn how to be a superhero." The voice paused. "Sadly, most of you won't apply the lessons or reach your true potential."

An audible gasp spread from student to student. Some demanded refunds, while others asked what true potential was. After several tense seconds passed, the questions died away.

The voice continued. "If you want to leave, you may. However, once you drop this class, you may not return. Each student has one chance at Superhero School. But if you stay, expect hard work. Every idea and moral will be questioned. The limits of your physical and mental abilities will be tested."

Low whispers flooded the room, but no one walked out.

● ● ●

Simon's mind was a whirlwind of possibilities. He could see his future: his battered coat and vest replaced with a shiny new suit and cape. He wanted to be pushed to his limits, tested against every other student. He knew he was stronger, faster, and harder working than anyone.

Impatience simmered in his belly. Talking just wasted time. Didn't they get it? This was more important than anything they'd ever learn!

The teacher's voice droned. She reviewed lessons and assignments. A schedule flashed onto the screen.

Simon was bored. He envied the llama's ability to nap through the whole class. Too excited to sleep, Simon studied his classmates, guessing their strengths and how he could take advantage of any weaknesses.

As much as it hurt to admit it, the twin cats oozed heroic attributes. Tall, muscled, and sleek, they would make tough opponents for anyone. Brains might be another story, but these two looked as though they took their physical training seriously.

Simon immediately dismissed other students. The pig was so round and clumsy, she wouldn't be stealthy or agile. The frog was puny and green—so green he glowed. That made stealth an issue too. Neither would win any contest for brawn.

He was sizing up Catt's abilities against his own when he was jerked back to the teacher's voice, saying, "...until the moment of truth. But we'll discuss that later."

The screen flickered, then steadied. A list of rules appeared.

"Each student signed a class agreement. We will review that agreement together, then take a fifteen-minute break. 'Number one: We will conduct ourselves respectfully and courteously at all times...'"

● ● ●

The teacher's voice buzzed like a fly inside Catt's ear, reciting rules with robot-like precision. Catt read the three-page copy that appeared on her desk. How or when it was delivered, she couldn't say.

"Class will resume in fifteen minutes," the teacher said.

Catt watched students rush out of the room for the break. Only Simon stayed. He waved at her papers, encouraging her to finish reading, then he sat back, crossed his paws over his vest, and settled in for a long wait. Catt read over the enrollment forms and rules.

Chatter filtered through the open door. Simon peeked over Catt's shoulder. She was stuck, rereading the same paragraph over again. Each pass drew more life from her face. Her chin quivered, and fat tears streamed along her nose, dripping onto the page.

● ● ●

Catt read rule number five again and again. It still hadn't changed:

> All students must complete a full family history report before attending school. A family's support is necessary for any superhero to succeed. Failure to provide this information will cause the student to be removed.

Catt wondered how she could provide information she didn't have. Her stomach rolled, and her paws felt sticky. Superhero School was more than she imagined. How could something so wonderful be given and yanked away so soon? Catt couldn't give this up. But how to explain her family history? She needed to find a way around rule number five.

Maybe she could talk to the teacher? But there wasn't an actual teacher to talk to, only a voice. The classroom was empty except for her and Simon.

Simon. Maybe he knew who to talk to...

If she resolved rule number five, today would be her best day ever! She had a new friend and a perfect school in a new and perfect place. Catt was going to be the best superhero student. Here she would learn to be helpful and respectable. And it was all thanks to Simon, her new best friend.

• • •

Catt flipped to the last page and scratched her name on the line. Her handwriting was terrible, but she would work on that. She gathered the papers and gestured for Simon to follow.

Catt pushed past the students crowded around the classroom door. When she started to ask Simon for help, he shook his head and pointed away from the crowd. He scurried down the corridor, far enough away that no one could hear them.

"Catt? What's wrong?" Simon asked, brushing his paw against her leg. His brows formed a deep vee over his long snout.

Catt closed her eyes and let her head rest against the wall. "I'm not like you, Simon. I can't give the school a family history because I never had one." She slid her toe across the cool tiles.

"Can't we talk to someone?" Catt asked. "I can't not go to this school!"

She slumped against the wall. "How can they expect me to say what I don't know?"

Simon considered Catt's problem. She didn't belong anywhere or to anyone. She didn't have a name—she didn't know who she was. She didn't have anyone she could trust, and she didn't even trust herself.

And yet Catt was asking Simon for help.

He felt ten feet tall.

Simon couldn't let her down. He needed to keep Catt enrolled at Superhero school.

But how?

He paced the slippery tiles as he brainstormed. Catt needs a family... I have a family... That's it!

=^.,.^=

Chapter Six

SIMON'S GRANDMA WHISKER loved a project. And Catt would be a big one. If he convinced Grandma to adopt her tonight, then Catt would have an instant family and their history.

Oh... But Catt was a cat. How did he forget that? Grandma Whisker would never tolerate a cat in the family.

Simon scratched his head. The answer will come, he told himself. The answer always came. He just sometimes had to coax it out of hiding. Think, Simon!

"I got it!" Simon snapped his fingers. Mrs. Gristle. Mrs. Gristle was an older cat without any family. She often took in strays at her big house. She could adopt Catt, and Catt could stay at Superhero School with him. They could be partners!

Wait a sec. Simon shook his head. Helping Catt was one thing, wanting to be friends was another. But to actually want to be partners at Superhero School? That was...impossible.

Maybe he needed a snack. Yeah. Low blood sugar caused hallucinations. That's all it was. He just needed to eat. No way could he trust a cat to be a friend or a partner.

Simon would have to do all the planning and more than half the work. Catt was lost and unsure. Not like Simon. He had big plans.

After Superhero School, he would defend Mouseville from bullies and enemies. Simon dreamed of a world without sadness, where nobody he knew got hurt or died because he didn't know how to help them. He would learn every superhero trick in the book. Twice, if he had to. His family and friends would stay safe on his watch.

And he would keep his superhero identity secret so he could be a regular mouse the rest of the time. It would be hard—the secret part anyway. How did superheroes do all those super things every day and not brag about it?

● ● ●

"Simon!" Catt hissed, trying not to draw attention from the students in the hall.

Simon blinked, coming out of his daydream.

"What?" he whispered.

Catt pointed at Room 207. Break time was up. The other students were returning to class.

Simon grabbed Catt's paw, tugging her down the corridor and past the door. It closed behind them, and the lights dimmed.

Catt tapped Simon's shoulder. "Do you have a plan?" she asked.

Simon waved the question away and pointed to the Superhero School logo on the screen.

"Tell me later," she whispered. Catt bit her nails and watched the clock on the wall.

● ● ●

Halfway through class, Catt's tummy shook. A slow rumble churned in the pit of her stomach, rose up her throat, and pushed past her pressed lips, erupting with a loud growl.

She tried to keep her face calm as she scanned the room with everyone else, searching for the source of the noise. No way would she let anyone know it came from her. Her cheeks flushed, but she kept her head up and shrugged at the pony in the desk next to hers.

She couldn't remember when she'd last eaten. This morning? No, the gardeners had been outside the fish market this morning. She was scared of the gardeners, so she'd wandered off and ended up in this strange world.

It was past five now. The old fish peddler would have set her dinner next to the trash bins. Catt usually ate twice, once in the morning and once in the evening, except on gardening day. But she hadn't eaten since last night. She'd missed many meals where she lived before, when the humans forgot to feed her. But now that she sat in a quiet class, her hunger distracted her.

Catt stared at the chicken with her bag of grain and licked her lips. The chicken didn't offer her any, and Catt didn't ask. She tried focusing on the screen as she pressed her paws over her noisy stomach. She prayed the rumbles would quiet or stop, but they were growing louder and longer.

Catt started to slink out of her chair, but Simon snorted and shook his head. He dug in his pockets, then passed Catt a teeny snack. It wasn't even a mouthful. Just a thin sliver of cheese and a dab of peanut butter on a broken cracker.

Catt popped the entire snack into her mouth and swallowed it whole. Simon shook his head and laughed. She smiled back and licked a crumb from her paw. It wasn't filling, but she was grateful for anything.

● ● ●

The teacher's voice was brisk and matter of fact. "This week's assignment is to choose which superhero trait you believe is the most important and why."

The room erupted. "Cool homework!" "This'll be easy!" "I totally got this!" Boasts and cheers still hung in the air when the teacher's voice rang out again.

"Remember, I want to know why you believe it's important. I want an essay with examples."

Groans replaced the glee. Quiet blanketed the classroom as the students waited to hear more from their teacher. When the voice remained silent, the scape of a chair leg and the thump of a backpack broke the stillness. Other students followed suit.

"Study carefully," the voice suddenly crooned through the racket. "Consider flaws and weaknesses too. See you next week."

Several students stopped packing up to stare at the projection screen. The school logo had disappeared. The screen slowly refolded itself into the ceiling, the classroom door opened, and the lights brightened.

● ● ●

As though a switch flipped, all the students began talking at once. The noise was deafening.

The pig in the purple cape rose from her seat, as poised and graceful as a dancer. She left the classroom, ignoring the noise and chaos as if it weren't there, with the frog jumping at her heels. She looked like a superhero in that moment, and Catt wished for the same dignity and grace.

Simon's eyes held an odd twinkle, making him look pleased with his first superhero class. But Catt felt lost and afraid, like she had tumbled into a different universe. Which she had, she realized. Would she ever go back to her other life? Maybe she would someday visit California as a hero. If she could stay at Superhero School, that was.

She grabbed the enrollment papers from her desk.

This was going to be hard, she thought. But Simon always had a plan, right?

Speaking of, where was Simon?

"Simon?"

Chapter Seven

CATT CAUGHT SIMON walking from the Community Center down a new street.

"Simon," she puffed. "Where are you going so fast, and what is the plan?"

Simon scampered down treelined streets. He occasionally paused to dig in a garbage can beside the curb. Once he found something, he shoved it into his pocket and hurried to the next can.

Catt was completely lost in this neighborhood. Plus she needed to eat, and soon. That bite of cheese and peanut butter was a short-lived memory to her empty stomach.

Simon rounded a corner, then strolled up the sidewalk to a tall yellow house. Catt was suddenly on edge.

Cats lived here. She could smell them. A lot of them.

This wasn't a safe place for a mouse.

● ● ●

Simon skirted the house and scanned the bushes casually, as though unconcerned about lurking cats. Catt released the breath she had been holding. No other cats that she could see.

Sniffing the air, she detected a food dish on the back porch. She thought she smelled tuna. Had Simon brought her here for dinner?

He must be terrified. A stray-cat refuge probably wasn't on his list of after-school hangouts. Especially now that it was almost dark.

Simon acted calm, but Catt noticed him checking the shadows as he approached the side door. Catt hid behind the nearest bush, her school contract rolled behind her back. Multiple cats meant potential fights. Not a good outcome for a single mouse.

Simon shoved himself through the swinging pet door and into the house beyond.

Catt froze, anticipating Simon's screech for help. She'd never seen a mouse use a cat door before.

He leaned the top half of his body back through the door. When he finally spotted Catt, he urged her to follow with an impatient wave.

"Come on, Catt! We don't have all day," he squeaked, then disappeared.

She looked wistfully toward the dish of tuna. She swallowed, making a meal of her fear, then pushed through the door to find Simon.

● ● ●

The kitchen—warm, clean, and fragrant—glowed despite the dark. The smell of a tasty dinner still hung in the air, making Catt's tummy growl. Her nose twitched as she hunted for any small bits left on the floor. But the floor gleamed, as clean as the tile counters and as empty as the wooden table beside the window.

"Psst!"

Catt's ears swiveled toward the sound.

Simon stood halfway down a dark hallway, leaning against a door jamb. A soft light pooled around him.

"Catt, in here." Simon pointed his thumb to the room behind him.

The room felt warm after the chilly walk from school. A single lamp cast shadows into the corners. Shelves climbed to the ceiling on two walls, each one covered with thick carpet pieces. Scratching posts, arranged by height, lined the floor in front of the shelves. Fluffy blankets, piled taller than Catt, stacked up next to a cluster of brand-new pet beds, still with their price tags dangling.

Where had Simon brought her?

She blinked twice to make sure she wasn't dreaming when she spotted the treasure chest, overflowing with ribbons, balls, string, and feathers on sticks!

Simon had found a cat paradise. Toss in a few mice to chase, and—

Catt halted her runaway mind. She couldn't chase mice anymore! What if she accidentally ate Simon's cousin or great-uncle?

Cat paradise indeed, but she felt so out of place here. This was Simon's world, not hers. Still, she couldn't wait to dive into that bulging box of toys.

With wide eyes, Catt scanned every nook and corner until she landed on the perch attached to the window.

The oldest cat she had ever seen stretched across the throne-shaped lounge.

Its fur was black and tan with splotches of white. It leisurely licked one delicate paw, not once looking up to greet them.

Catt looked at Simon. His face lit with a silly grin, he waggled his eyebrows.

The old cat spoke quietly, still grooming. "Hello, Simon."

Catt's head jerked up at her voice. Something about it sounded familiar.

"I see you've brought a friend." She flicked her tail and waved a white paw at Catt. "I'm curious. When did you two meet?"

Simon chuckled. "Well, I was falling out of the sky this afternoon—"

"I'll wait until our next visit for that story," she interrupted.

A tense quiet fell over them while the old cat's eyes tracked her visitors, eventually pinning Catt with a steely blue stare. Catt felt she was being measured when the old cat narrowed her eyes. Falling short once again, she thought.

The old cat flexed her nails. "Only an emergency would bring you here this late. You're keeping me from my beauty sleep, Simon, so get on with it."

Catt watched as she cleaned each paw, looking indifferent if not for the constant swish and flick of her tail. The old cat was annoyed and trying hard to hide it. Why? Catt wondered. Was she really so tired?

Simon looked worried, and that worried Catt. If Simon was afraid, she needed to look for the exit, and fast.

Simon's throat bobbed. "Mrs. Gristle," he began.

Mrs. Gristle. Her name was Mrs. Gristle, otherwise known as Mrs. Gee.

● ● ●

Mrs. Gee's gaze swung between the two as Simon explained Catt's problem at Superhero School. Simon finished his speech with a remarkable offer.

"Mrs. Gee, if you adopt Catt, she'll have a family and the family history needed to stay in school. In exchange, Catt will do anything you want."

What!

Catt glared at him. He stepped closer to Mrs. Gee, leaving Catt to stare at his back.

Do whatever she wants? For how long? What if she wants me to do something embarrassing or disgusting?

Catt didn't know Mrs. Gee. She didn't really know Simon either.

She couldn't tell if this was all a joke or if she were being sold to Mrs. Gee. Either way, she felt sick. She'd had owners before, and look what had happened. They'd dumped her, alone and hungry.

Coming to Sweet Meadows, she had thought, would solve all her problems. But now she had new, more complicated problems, and she refused to be property again. Maybe this wasn't the best place for her...

But then Catt remembered how kind Simon had been. Even when he didn't know her or if he could trust her, he still offered his help. She rubbed the singed whisker on her cheek.

With everything happening so fast, she needed time to think. Simon's plan would change her life again, and Catt would have to live with it.

She tried to make another plan, but this seemed to be her only option. Catt was an uninvited guest here. But Simon knew all of Sweet Meadows and everyone in it. Trusting him was her only hope. If he thought this was their best bet, then he was right. She could either take a chance with Mrs. Gee and go to Superhero School, or she could go back to being an alley cat.

● ● ●

Mrs. Gee held up her paw, and Simon hushed.

Her nose wrinkled as she studied Catt.

Catt held her breath.

"I'll do it," Mrs. Gee said, "on one condition."

Simon pumped his fist in the air. "Whatever it is, we'll do it!"

"No, Simon." She pointed a sharpened nail at the mouse. "It may be your plan, but it's not your choice. Catt must want to live with me."

Mrs. Gee glued Catt with a hard stare. Catt felt her face heat up.

"Well…" She didn't want to choose. She'd rather run away. But if she had to decide, she would. Superhero School was on the line.

Catt nodded, and her voice sounded stronger. "I'll do it."

"You don't know what I want yet," Mrs. Gee purred. Straightening her nightgown, a wicked glint lit her eyes.

Catt wondered if she would regret this later.

"Whatever it is, I'll do it," she said, and her stomach dropped to her toes.

● ● ●

Mrs. Gristle watched Catt sit with shoulders slumped and eyes cast down. Someone had broken this young cat's trust. That wouldn't be an easy fix, but Mrs. Gee always enjoyed a challenge.

She tilted her head to one side. "Now, Catt," she said, "you belong to me."

Chapter Eight

SMILING AND SATISFIED, Simon clapped.

Catt only managed a weak grimace. Her dreams waited to be crushed.

Mrs. Gee roamed the room, touching feathers and bells. "Catt will take breakfast with me every morning for one hour. Then she can take care of a few chores. Nothing too difficult. Just one meal and a few odd jobs. I could use some more help around here." She raised one brow at Catt. "Do we have a deal?"

Catt looked to Simon.

He flashed her a toothy grin and two thumbs up. He nodded at Mrs. Gee and gestured at the treasure-filled room, as if saying, How could you say no to this?

Could Catt trust them enough to accept their help?

"Ok—okay," she stuttered. The ice inside her heart melted a bit. "Yes. Thank you."

● ● ●

"Wonderful!" Mrs. Gee clapped, then pressed a button on her nightstand. "Nigel," she spoke into the intercom on the wall.

"Yes?" A deep voice flowed from the speaker.

"Bring some dinner for my guests and a bowl of warm milk for me."

Mrs. Gee waved them to a small table encircled by fat cushions. "Sit!"

Simon and Catt practically jumped at the sharp order.

Mrs. Gee softened her voice. "Nigel won't be a minute, and I hate eating by myself. Guests are such a treat!" The fine lines around her eyes crinkled.

They sank into the soft cushions, wiggling deep to get comfortable. A brown and black meerkat entered, dressed in a tuxedo coat and tie. He carried three bowls on a tray. The scent of gravy enticed Catt's nose.

The butler carefully placed each bowl on the table. He never looked at either Catt or Simon when he bowed, nor when he hurried out with his empty tray held up on one scrawny paw.

● ● ●

Catt's stomach reacted as the fragrance drifted from her nose into her empty tummy. She wondered, if she tickled Simon, might she snitch some from his bowl? He was itty-bitty compared to her, and he didn't need as much.

But she mustn't forget her manners. Manners would be important to Mrs. Gee, she was sure. She'd wait until their hostess gave them permission to eat. Catt rubbed her growling stomach and hoped it wouldn't be long.

"About this school," Mrs. Gristle said. "Are you in the same class? What's it like?"

Catt groaned at the delay. Simon grinned at her, then proceeded to answer in detail Mrs. Gee's every question.

Catt knew she would pass out from hunger. Simon wanted to play games now? Was that it? He seemed to enjoy watching Catt squirm.

She didn't listen to her table mates discuss Superhero School. The smell of warm gravy made tears leak from her eyes and saliva pool on her tongue.

Catt was so hungry.

Forcing herself to be patient, Catt sat up straight and pressed her lips tight. Even when all she wanted was to grab her bowl and pour the gooey goodness down in one greedy gulp, she held back.

She feared her tongue would fall out and drool would slide off her chin. It was torture. Catt was sure she would die before they stopped talking.

"Right, Catt?" Simon asked just as her tummy gave a loud growl.

● ● ●

Mrs. Gee laughed, bell-like. "I think Catt is too hungry to talk!"

"She might've missed a meal or two today," Simon said. Smirking, he dipped one paw into his bowl and licked the gravy off.

Catt was so hungry, she didn't notice his teasing.

"Simon!" Mrs. Gee scolded. "Don't pick on her. She's so weak, she can't defend herself. Go ahead, my dear."

Mrs. Gee nodded at Catt's bowl. She lapped around the edge, determined to be polite and unhurried. But, her hunger too far gone, she picked up the bowl and poured the entire contents into her mouth.

After licking it clean, Catt set the empty bowl down and tried to smile. Her full stomach bounced, then a thunderous burp flew out. Catt's ears flattened against her head.

Simon laughed.

Mrs. Gee's lips parted, but no words came out.

● ● ●

Catt's face and neck felt hot. She hung her head, not wanting to see Mrs. Gee's disappointed face, or Simon's smug grin.

This was no way to repay Mrs. Gee for taking her in. Why had she gulped her food like a stray? If she'd just taken her time, nothing bad would've happened. But Simon's stalling had nearly killed her, and now she wished she were anywhere but here.

Catt finally raised her head to look at Simon and Mrs. Gee. Their mouths hung open, with laughter and surprise. She wanted to sink into the carpet and disappear forever.

What if they changed their minds about helping her? What if Mrs. Gee didn't adopt her? No one else would want her either. And Simon. He knew she was hungry, but he'd kept talking and taunting.

Catt thought about all the good things that happened today because of Simon. Superhero School. Mrs. Gristle. None of it would've happened without him. Catt owed Simon. And Mrs. Gristle too. Her heart sank.

● ● ●

Simon and Mrs. Gee exchanged glances, then burst into laughter. They pointed at each other, then Catt, and howled.

Catt hated being laughed at. She'd rather be tossed in a pen of dogs than be made fun of.

"What's so funny, huh?" She stood with wobbly knees. "I ate too fast. It happens."

She flicked her tail and left the room.

The shrieking laughter followed Catt down the hall and out the door. She sat on the porch step.

Her bottom lip quivered. Her eyes stung as fat tears rolled down her cheek. A sob pushed past the lump in her throat. Her shoulders shook, her breath hitched, and her nose ran. Catt cried over every disappointment in her life. For messing up. For missing Simon. For being so unlovable.

She felt her mind teetering on the edge of something important—something that could change her life…or slip away forever.

All her dreams crumbled to ash. Mrs. Gee wouldn't adopt her. Superhero School was unattainable. And Simon…she supposed memories of her first and only friend would fade eventually.

Maybe she didn't belong in Sweet Meadows after all. She should go back to California. At least there, she knew what she had.

Nothing.

No one.

And that was the way it would stay.

● ● ●

NO! Something inside her didn't want her to give up.

Catt wiped the tears from her fur. She loved Sweet Meadows. It was her home now. She didn't want to go back to California. She wasn't going back. She would stay and fix her relationships so she could graduate Superhero School.

She needed to stick to the plan.

Simon would help her.

Oh…but Simon wasn't her friend anymore. Catt had been counting on him, but counting on others had never gotten her anything.

She could do this on her own.

Chapter Nine

CATT WAS STILL drying her tears when the pet door squeaked behind her. Simon's spindly feet curled over the step beside her.

Stars began to light the sky. Simon stared into the darkness, looking as though he tasted bitter medicine.

Mrs. Gristle sat on the other side of Catt. "Catt, we're so sorry." She smoothed a stray tuft behind Catt's ear.

"We didn't mean to make you cry. We were being too serious, and we needed something to break the tension. You helped us lighten up." Mrs. Gee offered a small smile, and Catt leaned into her gentle touch.

Simon nodded in agreement. His sad eyes pleaded with Catt to forgive him.

"It feels good to laugh," Catt said. She laughed herself and wiped her nose.

"That burp caught me off guard, and it was funny!" Mrs. Gee ducked to hide her smile. "It was never you we were laughing at." She raised her head to pin Catt with sparkling blue eyes.

"We don't think less of you because you burped. For heaven's sake, I do it all the time. With Nigel's cooking, I can't help but gobble it down too fast." Mrs. Gee's ears turned pink. "I know you think I'll change my mind. That all this will go away. But that won't happen. You're family now. My family. And I protect what's mine." She paused and looked at Simon. "That includes both of you."

Mrs. Gee's words lingered on the porch steps long after she shuffled back inside the house.

Catt tried to take it all in. She couldn't believe this whole crazy, fantastic day! She knew her future had changed, again, for the better.

● ● ●

Simon elbowed her. "Still friends then?" he asked, grinning lopsided and waggling his eye whiskers.

Catt laughed. She laughed until tears ran down her face. Now she was crying, but for a happy reason. She felt free and lucky for the first time. This morning, she had started with nothing. Now, she had more than she ever imagined: a friend who was odd, smart, and resourceful; a beautiful home; a family with Mrs. Gee...

And Superhero School.

Without thinking, Catt grabbed Simon around his waist and squeezed as hard as she could.

"Thanks, Simon," she squealed. "I'm so happy, I could sing!" Catt launched into song, her voice cracking, screeching, and flat. Down the street, dogs howled in protest, but she only sang louder.

Simon covered his ears. He pushed at Catt's limbs, which were banded around him. One hard shove, and Simon jumped to his feet. He raised his hands and stepped back.

"What the heck, Catt!" he yelled, and the barking dogs broke off. He dusted imaginary germs off his coat sleeves.

"Warn a guy, would ya! I've got a reputation, and it don't include hugging."

Catt tried to apologize, but every time she started, she ended up laughing again. He was trying to look furious, but she knew he was embarrassed. Now she knew she could embarrass Simon. She would keep that information tucked away for later.

● ● ●

Simon stopped fidgeting with his clothes long enough to say good night and remind Catt to give Mrs. Gee the papers to sign. He'd be back tomorrow after breakfast.

He stalked down the sidewalk, out the gate, and into the night.

Simon's reminder made Catt's heart flutter. Where had she left the papers? In the bushes? She couldn't remember, but she hoped Simon's plan would work.

A jaw-cracking yawn prompted her to twist and stretch. Oh, well, I guess I'll look for them in the morning, she thought. Smiling to herself, she skipped into her new home, happier than she could ever remember.

=^.,.^=

Chapter Ten

A DELECTABLE SMELL wafting from the kitchen made Catt's tummy rumble. She was hungry, but not starving like every other morning.

Last night when she'd come in, Nigel showed her to her room. It was a cozy closet, just big enough for Catt. A comfy bed with fluffy pillows and a soft blanket took up one half of the room. On the other side, a private litter box with automatic disposal and bowls of fresh water and warm milk waited for her.

After lapping up her milk, Catt groomed and used her new box. It was the best night's sleep she'd had in a very long time.

So much had changed yesterday, it was tough to imagine what would happen today.

Catt hurried to Mrs. Gee's door and knocked softly. She didn't want to wake Mrs. Gee if she was still sleeping. Cracking the door, she found Mrs. Gee exercising to music— at least Catt thought it was exercise. Mrs. Gee also sang along, off-key.

Catt covered her ears when she opened the door.

She didn't want to laugh at Mrs. Gee, but her morning workout was hilarious. She shuffled and swirled around the room, bumping into and stumbling over upturned boxes and strewn toys. Catt could tell she'd been active for a while by the state of things.

Catt laughed so hard, she fell onto her back, holding her side with one paw and covering her mouth with the other.

Mrs. Gee braked, one foot in the air, to watch Catt writhe and giggle on the floor. She winked at her, then continued to groove in perfect rhythm.

"Come in, dear. Want to jump in? It's really fun, not to mention good exercise." As awful at singing as Mrs. Gee was—and most cats are—her dancing was impeccable.

Catt didn't want to sound rude, but she hated exercise. The giggles having finally subsided, Mrs. Gee marched over, grabbed her paw, and dragged her into the room.

Catt followed her commands and, with a little encouragement, was soon prancing, swaying, dipping, and twirling beside Mrs. Gee. They laughed, grunted, and panted for half an hour, after which Nigel appeared with two frosty glasses of lemon water. Nigel's tray also held a pot of tea and bite-sized bagels layered with cream cheese and paper-thin slivers of salmon.

Catt grabbed a glass and let the tart liquid soothe her dry throat. Mrs. Gee drank hers down in one gulp, then waved a paw at the tray.

"Help yourself. I'm starving after that workout. I might wrestle you for the last bagel!"

Mrs. Gee placed two on her plate, poured a cup of tea, and sat on the floor. Catt piled the rest of the bagels on a plate, balancing it while she poured her own cup of tea.

They ate quickly and quietly. When Catt finished, she noticed Mrs. Gee's empty plate and cup on the tray. Catt stacked her dishes on top and waited for Mrs. Gee to tell her what to do next.

Mrs. Gee let out a soft, lady-like belch behind her paw. Catt looked away, but Mrs. Gee laughed. "Sorry. Couldn't help it. You know how it is." She pressed the button to call Nigel.

"Don't look so shocked, dear," Mrs. Gee said, noticing Catt's uncomfortable silence. "I've lived long enough to break a few rules. Besides, with Nigel's cooking, I eat much too quickly."

"Thank you for my room," Catt said. "And for breakfast."

Mrs. Gee smiled. "You're more than welcome. I like to keep extra in case a fellow cat needs a meal or a place to stay."

She paused and laid a finger across her lips.

"So, we need to get you enrolled. Nigel and I completed your school registration, as well as the adoption papers."

Mrs. Gee turned toward the door as Nigel entered. "You only need to sign the papers, and it's done," she said to Catt.

Catt's jaw dropped. Nigel carried a thin stack of papers that he set on the table, sliding the tray of dishes to the side.

Did Nigel find my school papers?

Catt signed her name where Mrs. Gee indicated on the adoption form, then again on the school contract, which was already filled out.

Mrs. Gee and Nigel signed after Catt. Nigel gathered the papers into a folder, then left with his tray. Mrs. Gee smiled at Catt.

"Welcome to the family!" She wrapped her arms around Catt.

Catt felt as if she were watching this happen to someone else. It didn't feel real. Her limbs felt heavy when she lifted them to return the hug.

I have a family.

Catt waited for the excitement she was sure she would feel, but it never came. This confused her. She wanted her heart to break open, but she didn't trust that it wasn't all a dream— that everything she ever wanted would be taken away. It was silly. She should be happy. She should feel relieved to belong somewhere.

But she didn't.

Seeming not to notice, Mrs. Gee shooed Catt out of the room for a bath and a nap, skipping the chores. Catt hoped that maybe then her mind would catch up with her feelings.

Chapter Eleven

CATT DREAMED IN the bright sunshine. She fought villains and defended the weak. After she saved Sweet Meadows, the mayor hosted a parade for her. Catt accepted the key to the city and was about to start her speech when she felt something thump her head.

"Caaattttt! Wake up!" A high-pitched voice jolted her upright.

"Catt, so help me, if you don't wake up right this minute, I'll find a firecracker and blast you awake!" Simon was so close, she could count the whiskers on his forehead.

She rubbed her eyes as the dream faded away. "Oh. Hi, Simon," she said, smothering a yawn. "I was taking a nap. When did you get here?"

"I've been trying to wake you up for five minutes! Must've been some dream. Where'd you go?"

"Sorry. I was just...um...chasing a mouse." Catt's face froze in horror as she clamped a hand over her mouth. What had she said? Blood rushed so fast through her veins, she expected her head to explode.

"Simon, I am so sorry!" Catt grabbed his limp paw and pressed it to her chest. "I don't know why I said that. It's not even true."

Catt squeezed Simon's paw before letting it drop between them.

"I was dreaming about being a hero. I was receiving the key to the city. That's why I didn't want to wake up. It felt so wonderful. I wanted to stay and enjoy the parade. You know… I didn't want you laughing at me again, so I made up the mouse story. I would never chase a mouse. Well, maybe before, but not now. What if I ate your cousin by accident? I'd never forgive myself!"

Simon chuckled, lightly at first, but soon he was roaring with laughter.

"Catt," he guffawed. "You're a CAT! You can't stop being a cat, and I don't want you to. It's only natural for you to chase mice." Simon sucked in a steadying breath. "But maybe you should meet my family…just to be safe."

He couldn't contain himself. Simon bent forward, laughing so hard he couldn't breathe.

Catt crossed her arms and tapped her foot. The two friends would have to deal with such crazy differences, and that would mean laughing at them. Finally, Catt let her arms fall to her sides, and she cackled along with Simon.

"Okay, Simon. Sounds like a plan. Lead the way."

● ● ●

Simon and Catt walked down the street, away from Sweet Meadows and toward the field, where they had met the day before.

"Speaking of plans," Simon said as he fished in his pockets. "I figure we're like a team. We should be partners, like Batman and Robin." He stopped rummaging long enough to look up at her. She stood with paws on hips, staring at him as if she'd never seen a mouse before.

"What do you say?" Simon asked.

"Partners?" Catt liked the sound of that. Simon was very smart and always prepared. While she was good at...um, well... She could be really quiet when hunting. Hmmm... She could climb really high. Oh, and she could run really fast if chased. Those were helpful skills. Right?

Simon saw Catt bite her bottom lip. "We'll be great," he said. "You'll see."

She chewed her lip, then made up her mind. She would learn how to be a super teammate.

"Okay, partners!" She flung an arm across Simon's shoulders but stepped back when he shuddered. Catt smiled to herself. Cooties or not, they were going to be superheroes together!

Chapter Twelve

"SO, PARTNER. WHAT do we think is the most important trait for superheroes and why?" Catt asked as they strolled along the gravel road toward Mouseville. "Do you think, since we're partners, the teacher will let us do one essay?"

Simon stopped. Suddenly, he was worried—not about their homework, but about how the residents of Mouseville would respond to Catt.

Simon hadn't thought this plan through. Mouseville's location was a secret. No one but those living inside the mouse village knew how to find it, and no one living inside the mouse village ever left it. They'd certainly never had a cat visit before.

Simon needed a plan to put the mice at ease and allow Catt to meet his friends and family.

Catt's question about their homework had caught him off guard. Could a mouse and a cat be partners in Superhero School? Simon couldn't guess, but he did know one universal characteristic of all superheroes: Courage. Doing the right thing no matter what. Some confuse courage with bravery.

Bravery is facing the things that scare you. But courage is putting others first.

Life was precarious for Simon. He wore fear like a comfortable shirt, never remembering a time when he wasn't afraid. Like leaving Mouseville to go to school or having a cat as a best friend. Simon figured he was brave, but courage was different. Could he give up his life to do the right thing?

Should he hide the fact that his new friend was a cat, or should he find a way to introduce her to Mouseville? It would be tough, but he knew what was right.

When Simon had the perfect answer to the homework question, he kept it to himself. "I don't know, Catt. I'll have to think about it. But right now, we have bigger problems."

"What problems?" Catt asked.

"No cat has ever entered Mouseville." Checking the road, Simon resumed walking. "There are rules."

She waited for him to explain, but he was picking up rocks from the side of the road.

"Here's my plan," he said. Catt leaned down to hear him better, but Simon lifted a rock over his head and smashed it against her temple.

"Ow!" she wailed. "Simon! What was that for?" She hissed when she touched the lump swelling above her right eye.

Simon examined the bump and released a low whistle. "Good."

"Good?" Catt cried. "Is this payback for the mouse thing earlier?"

Simon's strange grin made it look like he was handling something explosive. It was the same look he'd had right before he shoved that matchstick into her mouth. Catt didn't trust that look.

"All according to plan," he said.

"You planned to hit me with a rock? Are you insane?" Catt raised both paws over her head and let them fall. "It didn't work. Any other plans?" She mimicked Simon's weird smile.

"Actually, it worked quite well." That odd twinkle lit his eyes, and he explained the rest of his plan.

"Am-what?" Catt asked.

"Amnesia. Memory loss. From the bump on your head." Simon would say he found her wandering around and that she didn't know she was a cat.

This is crazy, she thought. No one will believe this. If this was his best idea, she was worried what the backup plan was. Because Simon had one, Catt was sure of that.

Simon laid out his plan, step by step. He would take Catt to Mouseville and convince the villagers that she couldn't be left alone. Since they were so close to Mouseville, he naturally brought her there for safekeeping until he found her someplace to recover.

All Catt had to do was act lost and confused. That would not be difficult, considering she had no idea what she was getting herself in to.

Then Simon listed the rules. Catt mustn't act like she wanted to eat, play, or chase anything. She must be gentle. No smiling—her teeth were too scary. No licking or grooming. No napping, pouncing, or sneaking. She mustn't flex her claws. No stretching, curling, or tail flicking. Ear swiveling was out too.

"Just act like a mouse, and you'll be fine," Simon said.

Catt practiced all the way across the field, picking up her feet and stamping, all while keeping her claws hidden. She felt like a wind-up doll, on the brink of falling. She got a headache trying to keep her eyes big and round.

But for Simon, she kept trying.

He barked orders every few steps. "Drop that tail. It looks like a flag. Cats do that, not mice! Let it drag behind you." He pointed out every flaw.

"Can you stand on your hind legs?" he asked. "Rub your paws together. Look around, nervous-like. Scrunch your nose and wiggle it."

Catt followed Simon's instructions, until he said she looked like she wanted to eat him. "Back on four feet then. I guess that will do."

Catt's head pounded as she marched toward Mouseville.

All at once, Simon stopped and whispered, "We're here. Keep acting confused. It's working."

Catt was confused. This wouldn't fool anyone. They should go back to Mrs. Gee's and make a new plan. Catt was about to tell Simon when he pulled back a thick vine and revealed the entrance to Mouseville.

Chapter Thirteen

MOUSEVILLE WAS BUSY. Mice scurried from hut to hut, each one small and tidy, made from twisted twigs and grass. Shiny leaves, overlapped like shingles, covered the roofs. Smoke puffed from chimneys. A large pot bubbled over a fire pit beside tables with tiny benches. The open walkway was swept clean and filled with working mice, reinforcing the walls. Shovels clanged, hammers banged, and mice children chased one another around the village.

All at once, they stopped mid swing, hammers and shovels falling to the ground. Their fingers pointed, and they whispered to one another behind their paws. Some of the females squealed. The male workers scowled and shook their heads. Others turned away when Simon called out and waved.

Every mouse in Mouseville stared at Catt, who was cowering just inside the entry. Her knees knocked, her heart pounded, and her blood roared with the rhythmic chant, Run, Catt! Frowns marked every whiskered face. The children hid, peering around skirts and woolen coats, eyes big with fear.

Catt tried to remember what Simon told her to do, but it tangled inside her head like a pile of spaghetti. She knew she would let Simon down. How did she get herself into these messes?

She swallowed hard, trying not to lick her lips. Each mouse moved in sync, like a well-trained army. Within seconds, every available broom handle, shovel, and pointy stick was aimed at Catt. A bell rang, echoing around the village and across the farms. The mouse militia advanced, ready to defend their homes from the cat.

● ● ●

Simon ran, his coattails flapping, to silence the alarm bell. He turned to address the approaching mice, waving his paws and patting the air.

"There's no need for that!" he cried. "Sorry to frighten you, but I need your help!" He paused until every eye was trained on him.

"My friend here—" He frowned, then laughed uneasily. "Um, by friend, I mean we just met. But she needs our help— uh, your help."

He looked from mouse to mouse, drawing out the suspense. "Seems she had an accident and hit her head." Simon rolled his eyes, revealing his personal thoughts on cats in trouble. Typical.

"She doesn't know who she is, what her name is, or where she lives."

A slow grin spread across Simon's face. He leaned toward the crowd as if sharing a secret.

"She doesn't know she's a C-A-T," he spelled out in a stage whisper.

● ● ●

The mice closest to Simon backed away. Others looked to their neighbors, confused. Simon must be joking.

70

Catt stood stock-still as shivers raced from her tail up to her ears. Simon would get her killed! She knew she was going to end up in that pot of boiling water before the day was over. Her stomach rolled, breakfast bubbling up in a greasy stew as fear blended with an overwhelming urge to use the litter box.

As Catt bounced from foot to foot, Simon paced in front of the crowd. "Of course, I thought of all you fine residents, here in Mouseville, with the ability to see past her upbringing and"—he cleared his throat—"species and offer aid to an unfortunate traveler."

Simon puffed out his chest and tucked his thumbs into the lapels of his vest. "The Mouseville I know and love would never turn away a hurting stranger."

Tiny mouse feet shuffled, and whispers raced through the crowd. "Why should we care?" called a voice from the back.

"I'm glad you asked. I need someone to watch over her until I can get back. She needs protection. She has no memory. It's dangerous out there and bad things happen to lost cats."

Simon lifted his paws. "Will anyone help me?"

Chapter Fourteen

CATT WATCHED EVERY mouse turn away from Simon. Her heart sank as she edged toward the gate. The mice returned to their chores, and Simon's shoulders dropped. Absently, he rubbed an ear and slapped his coat pockets.

His left paw bumped against a hard, round shape. Simon jerked his head up and called out to a lone young mouse, who was sitting against the front of a simple hut.

"Hey, Joe!" Simon walked toward the boy mouse, whose legs stretched awkwardly beside a pair of crudely made crutches.

Simon pulled a shiny blue disc from his pocket, letting it flash in the sunlight.

"Hi, Cousin Joe," he said, sliding down to sit beside the young mouse. "How's everything?"

Joe plucked the material covering his useless right leg. He scooted over an inch, making room for Simon.

Simon picked up Joe's crutches, checking the bindings and joints before setting them aside. "Soon it'll be time to make new crutches for you. You're growing tall."

Mouth twisted with envy, Joe watched the other young-sters skip and play in their yards.

"Whatcha got?" he asked, eyes finding the glittering sphere Simon rolled between his paws.

"Oh, this?" he held up the yo-yo up for a split second before it disappeared behind his paws. "Just something I found. You want it?"

The blue yo-yo sparkled when Simon held it out to Joe. All the mice—young and old—stopped what they were doing and watched.

Joe stretched out a trembling paw. His voice tightened to a squeak. "Yes."

Simon looped the string around Joe's finger. With Simon's directions, Joe let the yo-yo drop to dangle uneventfully at the string's end. After a few more tries, he had the yo-yo dancing up and down the string.

Eager youngsters edged closer, squeaking and shoving to watch the yo-yo roll up and down, guided by Joe. A beaming smile broke across his face. It was as if the sun peeked out on a cloudy day.

● ● ●

Joe's mother watched from the window of the hut, tears slid-ing down her cheeks. Wiping them away, she stepped outside.

"Simon?" She waited for her nephew to face her. She looked around, sheepish, then spoke out in a clear voice. "You know Joe will never walk again after escaping that hawk that took his father from us. We mice learn to never trust our enemies. But, Simon, I trust you. I know you wouldn't bring danger to our home." She looked doubtfully up at Catt. "I'll help her."

The toy clattered to the ground as Joe struggled to his feet, gathering the crutches underneath him. "No, Mom, let me do it."

The crowd hummed. Shoving mice aside, a thicker, healthier mouse squeezed his way to the front.

"Hey, Simon!" Chubby waved and walked to Joe's side. "I wanna help too! I'll make sure nothing happens to Joe, Mrs. Cheddar," he assured Simon's aunt before turning back to Simon. "And I'll take good care of your, um, C-A-T friend too."

A blush stained Chubby's round cheeks. He rolled a battered hat in his hands and dragged equally battered shoes through the dirt.

Simon laughed, patting Chubby on the shoulder. "You boys make me proud. I'm counting on you."

● ● ●

"SIMON CHEDDAR!"

An elderly mouse stood at the edge of the crowd, fists planted on skinny hips. She shook a finger at Simon.

"What in tarnation have you done? Bringing that thing here!" She waved her paw at Catt. "Have you lost your mind?"

Simon trudged toward the old mouse, embarrassment painting his ears red. She placed her paw against Simon's forehead, as though checking for a fever.

"Grandma, I'm trying to help out, just like you taught me." Simon tried to ignore the laughter from the other mice.

"Oh, you don't fool me for a minute, mister." She sniffed and pointed at Catt. "You got a plan, I take it."

Grandma Whisker's face softened with a slight smile.

Simon was a blur of words and paws as he explained to Grandma about C-A-T-S outside of Mouseville. How they had teased and bullied poor Catt before he could chase them away.

After a good deal of bragging, Simon shared his plan. He would go see Mrs. Gee, the cat lady, and arrange a safe place for the injured Catt. Until then, Mouseville was the safest place for her. If they kept Catt busy and out of trouble, he could go and return even faster.

The caretakers, who now included Grandma Whisker, agreed, and soon Catt waved goodbye to Simon, scarcely believing he had pulled it off.

Chapter Fifteen

"WHAT COULD POSSIBLY go wrong?" Simon had said.

The plan seemed to be working so far. Chubby, Joe, and Grandma took Catt to visit every home, business, nook, and cubbyhole in Mouseville.

Life was simple here. Catt didn't see the same technology as at Superhero School or the cell phones that Sweet Meadows townsfolk carried around. But it didn't seem to bother the mouse villagers. They were happy and hard-working.

Grandma Whisker entertained them with stories about her grandfather, Edward Whisker, who founded Mouseville. A fox had been chasing Edward when he discovered this very spot. He jumped into what he thought was a snarl of branches and instead found the most perfect, secluded home for his family and friends.

They moved in immediately, building the village almost overnight. Starting with thirty-five families, Mouseville today consisted of more than a hundred adults and dozens of mouse-lets. Grandma was the last of the original settlers still alive.

After the tour, the foursome headed to Grandma's house for lunch. Just as she pushed open her door, the village bell clanged a warning.

Residents slammed shutters, doors, and windows. Locking up tight, they huddled beneath tables and beds, quivering with fear.

Grandma waved Chubby and Joe inside, but Catt didn't fit.

Then the bell stopped as suddenly as it began.

Grandma Whisker stood outside the hut beside Catt, alert and trembling in the eerie silence.

● ● ●

They heard a slithering, hissing sound from behind the bakery. A tell-tale rattle followed.

Catt waited for directions from Grandma Whisker, but the old mouse was frozen, her face white with fear.

Catt saw the snake slither into the clearing. Its tongue flicked in and out, sensing for warm bodies.

Her hair stood on end. Simon had told her to act like a mouse, but if she didn't do something fast, that snake would gobble up Grandma and most of the village. Wishing she had one of Simon's trinkets or a clever plan in mind, she stepped in the snake's path.

Catt didn't take much comfort in being a cat, even if she did know how to defend herself from snakes. This was different. She couldn't just strike and run away. She had to defeat the snake. Mouseville was depending on her, and Simon would expect her to protect his family.

Digging her claws into the dirt, Catt puffed her fur, stretched her ears and tail, and gave a mighty yowl. She hissed, swiping at the snake's eyes.

Its tongue tasted the air as it watched Catt through slitted yellow eyes. It coiled itself and lunged at her, fangs exposed.

Catt smoothly dodged the strike, but that left Grandma Whisker unprotected.

Grandma lay face down with her paws over her ears. Her normally corkscrewed tail stuck out straight. Her dress billowed when the snake's tongue flicked at the loose skirt. Squeaks tumbled from her mouth when she felt it come and go. Glistening fangs dripped venom inches from Grandma's back.

• • •

Catt didn't think. She didn't make a plan. All she could see was Simon, angry because she'd let his grandmother die. He would never forgive her. He would order her to leave Sweet Meadows and Mrs. Gristle's house and Superhero School.

If Grandma Whisker died, Catt lost everything!

She sprung, claws out and teeth bared, onto the snake. Sinking her claws into the snake's body, she held on as it twisted and rolled. Then she bit the back of its thrashing head. A greasy, bitter tang coated her mouth. She gagged on the snake's skin, but she wouldn't let go. The snake tried to coil itself for striking, but Catt held on.

When the snake began to tire, she laid her full body over it. The snake bunched and stretched. Her jaws ached, but she knew what she had to do. Rising, with the snake clenched between her teeth, Catt whipped her head. With every snap, the snake twitched, until the head and body separated. Its body flew away and landed with a thud. Catt dropped the lifeless head and watched the last rattles of the tail.

• • •

As if in a daze, Grandma Whisker pushed to her feet. Doors and windows cracked open. And once again Catt faced a throng of shovels, broom handles, and sticks. Joe and Chubby stumbled over each other to get to Grandma Whisker. They were afraid.

Catt had killed the snake and saved Grandma and Mouseville, but now they feared her.

She dragged the snake's body, then the head out the front gate. No one said thank you. No one offered to help. No one said goodbye. No one said a word.

Simon was right. They had been friends before, but now she was a cat, and a cat was an enemy.

She waited outside Mouseville for a long time, hoping someone would come out to look for her. But the vines stayed shut with the mice concealed safe inside.

=^.,.^=

Chapter Sixteen

CATT SURVEYED THE empty road. She wished for Simon to show up with one of his crazy plans to make it all better. But Simon didn't come.

Eventually, she began the long walk home. Her feet felt heavy. Tears blurred the road ahead. Simon would be at Mrs. Gee's house...

Catt stopped crying. Simon was her friend, and Mrs. Gee was her family. They would help her. She'd saved Simon's grandma, after all.

Catt sprinted up the road and down the now-familiar sidewalk. She bounded up the steps and into the house. Calling out for Mrs. Gee, she searched every room, finding them empty.

When she rounded the corner to the kitchen, she bumped into Nigel. Cups and saucers rattled and crashed to the floor. A teapot broke and spewed hot water across the polished floor. Sugar cubes scattered like dice. The only unbroken dish, the cream pitcher, sat precariously on top of Nigel's bald head. The cream ran down his pointed nose and dripped onto his black tie.

Catt scrambled to stand, flinging broken pieces of china in every direction. She backed away from the mess, her paws outstretched, her eyes liquid and pleading.

• • •

Nigel grimaced. He raised one scrawny paw to wipe away the cream streaking his dour face. He spoke slowly and firmly, as though Catt were a child. "I can only presume there is a fire somewhere nearby."

Catt's breath whooshed out. Even surrounded by broken dishes and with cream dripping down his perfectly pressed suit, Nigel looked down his nose at her.

She couldn't suppress a snort. "I was looking for Mrs. Gee. Have you seen her?" She picked up the broken teapot, turned the tray over, and placed the broken pieces on it.

"Mrs. Gee?" Nigel sniffed. "I know of no one named Mrs. Gee. Is she new here as well?"

He looked behind Catt, as though this mystery character were lurking in the hallway. He looked irritated that a guest may have slipped past his notice.

"Nigel!" Catt giggled. "I call Mrs. Gristle Mrs. Gee."

"Why ever would you do that?" Nigel blinked, his wet whiskers dancing up and down.

"Because it's faster." Catt thought Nigel would scold her, but he straightened his tie, sniffed again, and declared that Mrs. Gristle was dining on the patio with Simon.

• • •

Catt watched Nigel stride into the kitchen, back straight, shoulders stiff, with a huge wet spot on the seat of his pants. Giggling to herself, Catt walked out toward the patio.

Mrs. Gee and Simon at first didn't notice her. Catt rehearsed what she wanted to say as the events at Mouseville replayed in her head. Slowing her steps, she worried how Simon would react. Maybe she should wait and talk to Mrs. Gee alone.

Simon's voice trailed off when he saw Catt on the patio. Mrs. Gee turned to see what held Simon's attention. When she saw Catt, she smiled and pointed to an empty chair.

"Catt!" she trilled. "What a wonderful surprise! From what Simon was telling me, I didn't expect you for hours. Come, sit next to Simon. Let's get a picture."

Mrs. Gee made them pose as she snapped pictures with her phone. "Smile, Catt! You look like you drank sour milk."

Finally, she rang a little bell for Nigel, then folded her paws into her lap. "So. Tell me. Was Mouseville everything Simon bragged about? I've never been. Obviously. But it must be so quaint!" Mrs. Gee shifted to the edge of her chair and leaned toward Catt. "I would give anything to go. So, how was it? What did you do?"

Her questions pelted Catt like darts, and they kept coming. When Catt felt the iron slats of her chair digging into her spine, Mrs. Gee was still gushing. "Stories are what I live for. You must tell me everything!"

Simon, on the other hand, hadn't said a word yet. And Simon always had something to say.

He propped his chin against his fist and smirked. "Yes, Catt. Do tell us everything."

● ● ●

Catt's tongue, sand-paper dry, rubbed her lips.

"Why are you here and not in Mouseville?" Simon asked. "Did something happen? Did you not follow the plan, Catt?"

Catt forced herself to sit up tall and look them in the eyes. But when she tried to speak, the words stuck in her throat. She didn't want to disappoint Simon or Mrs. Gee. If only she could fix this without them knowing.

87

Without thinking, Catt pushed to her feet and dashed across the yard. She ignored Simon's and Mrs. Gee's shocked voices calling her name.

Blinded by tears, Catt sped up and down unknown streets until she found an empty alley, quite like the one where her owners had left her. She huddled on a box beside a garbage bin, letting every regret pour out in sobs.

Hours passed. Her quiet sniffles echoed against the narrow walls. Catt stroked her tail and hugged it to her chest.

The sun had set and the alley was dark. But she didn't know how to get home, it being too late to ask directions. She wasn't entirely sure she still had a home. By now, everyone would know what happened in Mouseville. Simon wouldn't be her friend, and Mrs. Gee wouldn't want her anymore either.

She was on her own…again.

=^.,.^=

Chapter Seventeen

A YOUNG MOUSE sneezed and scooted across the cold pavement, nearly smashing into Catt's leg. Motionless in the moonlight, it waited to be eaten.

Catt kept her movements small and slow. She didn't want to scare the poor thing to death. But she'd heard other strays picking through the garbage earlier and didn't want to leave the little mouse to their appetites.

She tucked him between her paws and curled her tail around to keep out the cold. After a while, the mouse asked why she hadn't eaten him. Catt told him about her friend Simon. About how brave and caring he was. Simon was her best friend, she said, even though cats and mice couldn't be friends. He always had a plan. And she told him how much she missed Simon.

When the mouse, who had a cold and whose name was Melvin, asked why she didn't go visit Simon, Catt swiped the tears away and stood.

She had spied part of a turkey sandwich in the dumpster. Catt dug it out and tore off pieces to share with Melvin.

Maybe she couldn't be Simon's friend, but she could still protect his kind, if just for one night.

● ● ●

Simon trudged down the dark road toward Mouseville. What had happened to Catt? She acted so strange at Mrs. Gee's house. He couldn't imagine what would make her run away like that?

He had been telling Mrs. Gee about how he convinced the residents of Mouseville to let a cat in. He had felt like he could do anything then. He felt like a superhero. Nothing was impossible.

He had been bragging, almost to the best part of the story, when Catt cut in. She had looked so sad. Even Mrs. Gee's questions about Mouseville hadn't cheered her up. When Mrs. Gee urged Catt to talk, she had only stared at Simon with red eyes. Then she ran away.

Why? Something must have happened in Mouseville to make her sad.

Just wait until he got hold of his so-called friends and family! Making his friend sad—cat or not—was not okay with him.

● ● ●

But what if he had made her sad? Had Simon hit her head with that rock too hard? What if Catt had really lost her memory? Had he made Catt afraid of mice?

"Oh, Catt!" Simon groaned. He didn't feel super at all now. Simon had let his best friend down, and he didn't know how.

If he could find out what happened, though…then he could fix it. He could make it all right again. Then they could go back to being…uh, um…being…hmmm… Well, he and Catt were friends. And partners? So they would be friends and partners again. No, they were still friends. This was just a little misunderstanding.

When Catt hadn't returned by dinnertime, Simon worried. Catt's stomach ruled over everything. If she missed a meal, then she was in trouble.

He needed to find Catt. He couldn't have his best friend and his family on different sides. He needed both of them.

Simon swore that he'd stop all the silly tricks and crazy capers and just be Catt's friend. He and Catt were perfect partners, and they would be the perfect superhero team. He just needed to get his family and his friend back on the same page.

For that, he needed a super-sized plan.

● ● ●

Grandma Whisker paced in the field outside of Mouseville. Her legs ached, and her stomach was empty and sour. She searched the darkened countryside for any sign of Simon. The crickets sang, but Simon's familiar form didn't appear.

Cook was washing his pans from dinner. He had been chopping wood for his fire when Grandma began her wait for Simon. Dinner or no dinner, she would wait for her grandson. She needed to deal out a serious talking-to.

Knowing he had caused the trouble would be painful for him. He worked so hard to take care of everyone in Mouseville, bringing home trinkets and the oddest inventions to solve problems and provide for their needs. But she couldn't avoid him or put it off until tomorrow. As village elder, it was her job to deliver the bad news.

After Catt killed the snake, two more cats attacked Mouseville. They demolished most of the homes, along with their few treasures. Her own hut, the one Simon was born in, was nothing but a pile of sticks and leaves.

Three brave mice had to be carried to Doc Molder. A broken foot, a torn ear, and one missing tail—all suffered to protect the mouse-lets. Everyone else shifted through the jumble of twigs that had once been their homes, looking for anything to save.

Simon had a lot to answer for. Mouseville had remained camouflaged for generations. Now, on the day Simon brings Catt here, they are attacked by two dangerous intruders? Simon's actions put the whole village at risk. Worse than careless, it was reckless.

Fear ruled where peace used to reign. Many residents wanted to move away, with more packing up their few belongings every hour. Grandma Whisker had seen bad times before, but nothing like today. Everything her family had built was gone. One minute they were happy and whole. The next, a heaping pile of shattered hope.

Because of Simon.

There was little doubt that Catt exposed their hideout to her fellow cats. After the snake invasion, she knew the villagers wouldn't be prepared to defend Mouseville twice in one day.

Simon had led cats right to the gate. For that betrayal, he would be made to leave and never return. He wasn't welcome by family or friends here anymore. The village had voted to banish him from Mouseville.

● ● ●

Plodding through the moonlit field, Simon wondered where his plan had gone wrong. He might be a silly dreamer to think that kindness could fix everything. He believed that even he, a simple field mouse, could change his small corner of the world by promoting kindness to everyone, no matter their status or species.

Simon was so caught up in his dreams, he didn't notice Grandma Whisker. Eyes blazing, she marched up to Simon with her paws on her hips.

He tensed. Something was very wrong. Grandma wasn't ever mad. Grandma wasn't ever outside the gates of Mouseville, especially after dark. In fact, she was usually asleep by now!

Tufts of Grandma's hair stood on end. Her dress snapped in the wind, her apron cracked like a whip. Her normally smooth voice grated Simon's ears. She held him at a distance with a paw on his chest.

He was stunned. Grandma never acted like this.

"I've been waiting for you, young man!"

● ● ●

"I'm here now. What's going on?"

Simon stepped back and straightened his sleeves and jacket. She shoved him back another step.

"Yes, you're here. After your 'friend' let you know the coast was clear, hmmm?"

Simon had never heard Grandma talk like that.

"No! I mean, what? What friend? What coast? What—are—you—talking—about?" Simon shouted each word. He was tired, and his grandmother was scaring him.

Simon wondered if she was sick. He'd heard about some old people acting crazy when they got sick. Be patient, he told himself.

"So that friend of yours didn't tell you?" Grandma sneered. "Can't say I'm surprised. Their kind being so sneaky and devious. I suppose she told you that she was your friend, right? And that she wouldn't dream of hurting another mouse, hmmm? Sound familiar? Because she understands us?"

Simon closed his gaping mouth, swallowed the hard lump in his throat, and squared his shoulders.

"Grandma, I know something bad happened with Catt today, but whatever it was, it's my fault—"

"BAD?" She sputtered and shook, slapping a paw inside the other each time she repeated the word. "Bad"—slap—"is when a dish gets broken! Bad"—slap—"is when a fight breaks out! This is so beyond bad"—slap—"that I don't know where to begin, Simon!" Grandma Whisker slapped her paws twice more, then balled them into fists.

Simon flinched and stepped back from her.

"What happened, Grandma? I'm missing something here." He raised one finger. "Catt ran away." He raised another finger. "You don't make any sense." Then he raised a third finger. "And I have a splitting headache from trying to figure out what happened when no one is saying!"

Simon was shouting by the time he finished and not caring who heard him.

Grandma Whisker looked Simon over. He was holding his head, his eyes popping.

"You really don't know, do you?" she rasped.

She sat wearily on the dry grass and patted the spot beside her. Simon lowered his tired body, one painful joint at a time. No one talked for a while.

With horrific detail, Grandma Whisker recounted the events of the day. She began with Catt's appearance in Mouseville and Simon's crazy story about forgetful cats. Then came the snake attack. Her voice shook when she revealed how the snake had cornered her. How Catt, with her swift prowess, had saved them all.

Tears collected in Grandma's eyes when she recalled how the mice turned their fear toward Catt. They had made her feel unwanted and unwelcome, and she ran away.

Then, when all was calm again, two new cats ripped through the gates. They slaughtered the guards, and it took no time for them to destroy the rest of Mouseville. This time, there hadn't been a hero to save them.

Then the gossip began. It picked up steam with every shovelful of debris. Mouseville was gone. They blamed Catt. She had planned the attack, they said. She pretended to have lost her memory to gain entry to Mouseville. When the snake attack revealed her true vicious nature, she was free to carry out her own plan. Her feline friends had waited nearby for her signal.

Grandma Whisker dabbed tears with the corner of her apron.

"Simon, what are we going to do? The council decided. They sent me to tell you to stay away. How do I say that? How can they make me do this?"

She stood with her back to Simon. "I'm sorry, grandson. You're not welcome in Mouseville anymore. We packed your things and set them outside the gate."

● ● ●

Simon sat on the ground, waiting for his grandmother to say something more. But when he looked back toward the ruined gates, Grandma Whisker was gone.

He rubbed his eyes, trying to escape this horrible dream. But no matter how much he rubbed, his cast-out belongings still lay outside the village.

It wasn't a dream. Simon was homeless and alone. He needed a friend to talk to. But Catt had run away. Grandma and the others had thrown him out like trash. Simon only had himself.

Chapter Eighteen

FROM THE DARKEST corner of the alley, Ricky Rent watched Catt cuddling the sick mouse and wished it were him. The narrow passageway seemed to welcome the bitter night winds. His feet felt frozen to the pavement, and a shiver rippled down his back. He had no one to curl into for warmth. These nights were hardest for mice like Ricky.

He focused his camera phone on Simon Cheddar's best friend, Catt, snuggled tight against another mouse. He clicked the button, saving another picture. His photos from today totaled forty-eight.

Later, safe in his dusty hideout, he would examine the album, reliving this record of his day. He would take time to scan every detail and appreciate his talent.

He had fifty pictures now.

It had been pure coincidence when he found Catt and Simon outside Mrs. Gristle's house yesterday.

The idea that Simon was welcome at the cat house burned deep in Ricky's belly. The strays who ate there wouldn't hurt Simon, but Ricky had a thin white scar down his back leg to prove he wasn't so lucky. He didn't understand why Simon wanted to hang around such disgusting Meadowians. Cats were filthy, mean, and lazy.

But Simon hadn't fought for scraps or for a few inches of living space. He wasn't like Ricky, who was scrimping and scraping to survive. Living behind Mouseville's secluded walls, Simon enjoyed comforts Ricky couldn't imagine. Safety. Peace. Family. Friends. Food. Simon was one lucky mouse.

City mice were born unlucky, and Ricky was as city as a mouse could be. His clothes smelled like the garbage he'd found them in. His fur lay in clumps, and his skin was red and itchy from fleas. His home was a small, cramped hole in the kitchen wall, where the neighbors—ants, who lived behind the stove—marched sleeplessly past his door, night and day. Ricky felt sure that never happened in Mouseville.

Simon, with his coat pockets full of tricks, thought he was so important. But Ricky knew Simon Cheddar wouldn't last a day in the city. He was too soft, too fat, too pampered. Ricky could live two years on Simon's coat alone. He was just as clever as Simon, and maybe more. He had to be clever to survive. Still, Simon got all the attention.

Soon, everything would be different for Simon. But Ricky didn't feel bad for him.

He snapped a few more pictures, ignoring his stiff fingers and rumbling stomach.

● ● ●

On the other side of the city, Buff and Bash slurped their dinner at the tavern. The twin Siamese cats continued to brag to a rapt audience. With every retelling more exaggerated, the twins celebrated their bold invasion and destruction of Mouseville, declaring the mission a success. Buff grinned wickedly, dabbing at imaginary tears for the now-homeless mice.

He paused, waiting until the laughter died, heightening the drama. Then he clicked glasses with Bash. "And...we made sure they blamed Catt for it. Here's to Simon Cheddar's new best friend!"

With the laughter roaring again, no one noticed the small green frog crouched beside the tavern door, nor when he hopped away.

• • •

Frederick Flickerson needed Patricia Porter. This news was red-hot. Finally, he had something worthy to bring her. Two Superhero School students framing another for vandalism! Freddy could already picture the pretty pig's wide smile.

Patty knew how to use information. Freddy never understood why she got teased. She was smart. Genius even. She could make any computer speak her language. Freddy was amazed with what she could do with just a phone.

"My babies," Patty called them. More like spoiled children, Freddy thought. Freddy tried borrowing Patty's phone once. He never made the mistake again. She acted as if he'd broken it. His ears still rang from the lecture she'd given him.

Freddy hopped down Miller Farm Road toward Patty's barn, wondering if she would be in a good mood today. Some days, when she was being teased, she was bad-tempered. But she couldn't help being a pig. Too bad no one besides Freddy could see past that. He wished the world knew the shy girl he adored, who loved to sing and dance when she didn't know her frog friend was watching her from the corner.

He'd loved Patty from the moment they'd met.

Buff and Bash had trapped her that day, calling her "Fatty Patty." Freddy had jumped between them, which only turned the attention away from Patty to himself. The twins had followed him, snickering and insulting. They made Freddy feel smaller than he already was.

Then Patty had thanked him for sticking up for, and they'd been friends ever since.

Although intelligent, Patty was distracted by her work. So Freddy took care of her. When she forgot to eat, he made her smoothies. He kept her refrigerator stocked, her phones charged, and her days interspersed with fresh air and exercise. Freddy knew they were perfect for each other.

● ● ●

Patricia Porter wiggled in her seat, feet and hips bouncing to the music. Her hoofs flew across her computer keyboard. She'd hacked into the Community Center's main system. Determined, she scanned file after file for the Superhero School instructor's identity.

Nothing.

Every file led to another to another, but no mention of a name. The computer only referenced code "CW01" over and over again. But Patty couldn't find what the code symbolized. It was as if it didn't exist. But that couldn't be. The information had to be somewhere in the files, and Patty would find it!

Scanning the available data, she focused on one small record, almost hidden. Teacher Contracts and Payments. "Aha!" She clenched her teeth, hoofs a soft blur over the keys. Then she opened the document and scanned the names and accounts.

"That's odd—"

Thump! The door slammed against the wall. Patty jolted, banging her head on a lamp. She closed her laptop and greeted Freddy with a sheepish smile.

● ● ●

Freddy slouched against the doorframe, chest heaving. His tongue licked one red-and-gold eyeball, then the other.

Patty poured Freddy a glass of water. Grateful, he tried to speak and sip, but it gave him hiccups.

"I have some—hiccup—news—hiccup." He took a breath and tried again.

"The twins, Buff and Bash, attacked Mouseville and blamed it on Simon Cheddar's friend Catt. Now no one knows where Catt is, including Simon."

Freddy's heart knocked against his chest as he watched Patty turn bright pink. She pulled out a briefcase and dumped its contents on her desk.

Patty was tired of bullies. Buff and Bash especially. But this didn't make any sense. Why would they do something so vile, brag about its brilliance, then blame someone else? Buff and Bash always wanted credit for the pain and suffering they caused. Why would they blame Catt?

No one knew anything about the new cat. She showed up at Superhero School with Simon—no family, no history. It was as though she hadn't existed before that day.

Something strange was going on here, but information was power. Patty opened her computer again and began her search.

=^.,.^=

Chapter Nineteen

SIMON WATCHED THE sun rise as he walked to Sweet Meadows. It was early, before the birds sang, before the squirrels rushed about, before the mice of Mouseville woke up.

Simon had spent the night huddled with his belongings outside Mouseville's gate. He waited for Grandma Whisker or Joe or Joe's mother to come out—anyone who might still be on his side—but no one ever did, so he marched into town.

He needed to find Catt. All night he'd sorted through the facts, but he couldn't make them straight.

Catt wouldn't. She couldn't. She could barely feed herself, how could she organize and execute such an elaborate plan? Then why go to Mrs. Gristle's house after? She knew Simon was there. Besides, if she did actually plan it, why wouldn't she stay to make sure it worked?

She was acting odd at Mrs. Gee's house, though. And she'd run away. She'd even cried. Maybe she had done it and then felt bad about it.

Simon shook his head. Did she do it, or didn't she? Simon couldn't decide. He needed facts, and that meant asking Catt.

With every tired step, Simon wrestled between Catt his friend and the Catt Grandma Whisker had described. Both felt possible.

But that couldn't be right. There was only one or the other.

• • •

Just outside town, Patty paced around her barn, bumping tables and jostling dishes when she tried to squeeze between the furniture. All these facts didn't add up. Every problem had a solution, but the information needed to line up first.

Freddy hunkered beside the door, ready to rescue the next item before it fell. He loved watching Patty work.

She stopped, turned to Freddy, and ticked off facts, one at a time.

"First, Mouseville was attacked. Second, Buff and Bash are the attackers. Third—and this is where it stops making sense—they blamed Catt, yet they also bragged about it?" She rubbed her double chin. "Why would they go to all that trouble to blame Catt, then take credit for it?"

Freddy didn't answer. He wasn't supposed to. He knew she needed to ask questions to organize her thoughts.

"Another thing, Catt was nowhere near Mouseville when it happened. The photos posted by Mrs. Gristle on her Catbook account show Catt and Simon at her house that afternoon." Patty flipped through photos on her computer. "And the police report states multiple Mouseville witnesses who identified Buff and Bash as the perpetrators. The mice said Catt was in on it, and yet no one reported seeing her during the attack."

Frowning, Patty focused on the last few notes in the report. "Hmmm… It says here that a city mouse was seen earlier near Mouseville. Why would a city mouse be in the country? And on the very day Mouseville is attacked? Very suspicious."

Patty stared at the ceiling, sorting the facts through her computer-like brain. The pieces turned and realigned. One piece didn't fit. What was a city mouse doing in Mouseville? City mice and country mice didn't mingle. And when they did, it was likely a fight. Patty figured they both had their reasons, but communication and compromise solved most problems in her experience. Of course, neither side cared what Patty thought.

She shook her plump body. She was going off track.

The question was, Where is Catt?

• • •

Patty's nimble hoofs clicked across the computer keys. Freddy watched, fascinated, until she motioned him closer. She pushed back her chair and pointed to the video on her screen.

Grainy and dark, the scenes played, jumping every few seconds. Freddy cocked his head and shrugged.

Patty elbowed him away, clicked a few keys, and pointed to the monitor again.

Now divided into six smaller boxes, the video played again. Security feeds from the Sweet Meadows Police Department? Freddy's eyes widened. They had crossed a line here, but he didn't know how to stop Patty. She looked unfazed. Freddy held back a million reservations. He knew she wouldn't have done it if it wasn't important.

One square of security video focused on Catt, huddled in an alleyway behind the city deli. She was curled up with a tiny mouse, asleep. The next recording followed Catt from Mrs. Gee's house to the alley. Another showed the twins outside the tavern, still carrying on for the crowd.

Then Simon appeared in the next recording. The footage followed him from Mrs. Gee's to a field outside town. In the next scene, Simon argued with his grandmother. Then it switched to a live video of Simon walking toward the city.

They watched Simon stop at every shop, office, and café, presumably looking for Catt. They watched him walk until he was a few blocks from the deli.

Patty reached for the keyboard. A recording from the day before popped up. In it, Simon hit Catt with a rock!

Patty paused the video. With a stylus, she took notes on an electronic tablet, then clicked the play button again. Now they saw Simon and Catt disappear behind some vines.

"Mouseville," Patty said. Freddy nodded.

Then Simon left Mouseville without Catt. Patty scribbled on her tablet and fast-forwarded through the footage. Catt left a while later, carrying a dead snake. She buried the snake, then she ran toward Sweet Meadows, weeping. Patty replayed the video of Catt with the snake and took more notes.

She rewound and paused, jotted details and printed photos. When Patty shut down her computer, she collected the copies from the printer inside a folder marked "EVIDENCE."

"I have questions only Catt can answer," she said. She draped her purple cape over her shoulders and tied it at the neck. Stuffing her phone, tablet, and folder into a briefcase, she pulled the hood over her ears and set out the barn door.

Freddy followed Patty down the road toward the city. He hoped the deli was open. He was hungry, and Patty hadn't eaten breakfast.

Chapter Twenty

RICKY RENT HUDDLED between the dumpster and brick wall to stay warm. The morning sun was creeping into his dank corner, but it was still frigid. The smell of garbage and spoiled food hung in the air.

He rubbed his eyes and waited for Catt to wake up. The sounds of doors opening, trucks rumbling, and voices murmuring meant the city was waking up too.

Small footsteps, too faint for anyone other than a mouse to hear, came closer.

Simon. Ricky heard the other mouse's mumbling as he approached from the sidewalk. Ricky's teeth ground together.

"Well, well, well, the King of Mouseville," he said to himself. "Must be tough, now that you're the king of nothing."

● ● ●

Simon marched into the alley, paws curled, jaw clenched. Anger seeped from his every pore. Then he spotted Catt, still asleep and wreathed around a little mouse.

"Melvin," he breathed. His fists loosened. His shoulders relaxed. This was the Catt Simon knew—gentle and sweet.

Simon reviewed his plan. He'd planned to yell and demand that Catt tell him everything, but now he couldn't. Simon wouldn't shatter the quiet peace that surrounded the two sleepy misfits. He sidestepped scattered garbage, wrinkling his nose at the awful stench, to stroke Catt's ear.

He cleared his throat and shook her leg. "Catt?" he whispered. "Catt," he said louder. "CATT!" he shouted, his voice ringing off the brick walls.

● ● ●

Catt stretched, easing around Melvin. Her blinking eyes focused on a familiar face. She shook last night's dreams from her mind, but still, Simon stood before her.

Would the police come to arrest her soon? Catt looked around, but no one else appeared in the alley. She studied Simon's face, expecting to find hurt and anger. But he was smiling.

"What are you doing here, Simon?" she asked, stretching her toes. She didn't want to disturb Melvin, but she needed to uncurl her back.

"I know I'm the last one you want here, but I need some answers."

"I know." Her voice cracked. "I didn't know what else to do. I couldn't let that snake get your grandma. So I killed it."

She waited for Simon to retort, but he didn't.

"I'm not like you," Catt whispered. "I didn't have a clever plan. I'm sorry, Simon. I guess we won't be partners now. Tell Mrs. Gee and Nigel I won't be back. I'm going back to California." She closed her eyes, unable to watch Simon leave.

● ● ●

"So that's it?" Simon said through gritted teeth. "That's what all this drama is about? A snake?"

He stepped back, swallowed his anger, then began again in a softer voice. "Catt, we've got bigger problems. Did you know Mouseville was destroyed yesterday?"

Catt felt the blood drain from her head. Destroyed? But, but, but…the snake is dead. I buried it!

"Another snake attack?" she asked.

Simon chuckled dryly. "Sort of. A pair of snakes with paws and tails. Friends of yours? Hmmm?"

Catt's empty stomach churned. Friends? He meant cats. Oh, no. The day she's allowed to visit, and cats show up? That wasn't a coincidence. Mouseville believed she had betrayed the secret location of their village. This was worse than bad. Could she convince them she hadn't done it? Probably not.

Simon blamed himself. She saw that in his sagging shoulders and tired eyes. That lost look. This wasn't her confident, make-a-plan-on-the-spot friend, who fought for everyone and everything. This Simon had given up.

Catt needed to fix this. Simon had responsibilities—folks who were counting on him, not to mention a grandmother who loved him. He was a super leader, and Catt needed to help him remember that. Together they would avenge Mouseville and clear their names of guilt.

Chapter Twenty-One

PATTY AND FREDDY hurried into the alley. They crossed behind the deli as Simon sank to the ground, tired and defeated. The concrete looked cold and sticky beneath him.

Freddy hopped forward right away, but Patty waited near the sidewalk. She checked the corners, up above, and behind before she joined Freddy.

A prone Simon mumbled to himself. A wide-eyed Catt watched him with concern.

A flash from near the dumpster lit up the walls. Patty stared for a minute, then added notes to her tablet.

Freddy hopped around rotten bits of food, chewed gum, bent straws, and wet paper, then he disappeared under the dumpster. He wanted to see what had caused that flash. Freddy thought it could've been the sun reflecting off something metallic in the garbage pile. But all he found was a smelly mouse digging through the litter strewn under the bin.

● ● ●

Ricky aimed and snapped a few pictures before he tucked the phone inside his ragged shirt. The pig was curious. She looked right at him, as if she already knew he was there. Then she wrote on a tablet. But the pig hadn't seen him—she'd seen his camera flash. Ricky had forgotten to turn the flash off this morning.

But that stupid little frog almost caught him.

As a street mouse, Ricky was a pro at looking bored. He rummaged through the debris and ate rubbish. Not like it was the first time. He pretended not to know or care about what was going on around him. The act worked.

When everyone turned their backs to him, Ricky plotted. Somebody was going to pay for his cold, stinky, sleepless night.

● ● ●

Patty shuffled papers inside a folder. Swirling her cape, she cleared her throat for the third time before Simon and Catt looked at her.

"Uh, hello. I'm Patricia, uh, Patty. Patty Porter." She waited to be recognized but only got blank stares. "Uh, from Superhero School?"

She waved a hoof at the frog. "And that's Freddy Flickerson."

"Freddy, or Frederick, is fine with me," he said.

Simon and Catt blinked at them. Patty stamped her hoof and snorted. "We're here to help."

Simon shook his head. "Sorry, Patty, but we're kind of busy. Maybe later, okay?"

He turned away. When Catt stretched, Melvin sneezed and scurried under a box.

Patty stepped between Simon and Catt, laying photos on the ground. Security cameras had captured Catt leaving Mouseville, arriving at Mrs. Gee's, wandering around Sweet Meadows, and ending here in the alley.

Simon glanced at the stills from the security footage showing Catt's whereabouts yesterday. "We know all this. That's not helping."

"Wait!" Patty shouted. Red splotches stained her cheeks and ears. She pulled more photos from her folder, each with red circles.

"Look at these. Every image has this odd flash. It's a camera flash! Someone's following Catt and taking pictures. We need those photos and whoever took them. They know something!"

"Why would anyone want pictures of me?" Catt asked.

"Someone's always taking pictures," Simon said. "It doesn't mean they were taking pictures of you."

Patty rubbed her chin. "That's true, but I think she was followed." She looked pointedly at the street mouse digging through the garbage. "I think it was a mouse," she whispered, pointing a hoof beneath her crossed arms.

● ● ●

Ricky looked up as the foursome turned to stare in his direction. He grabbed his battered backpack and ran for the mouse hole behind the rusted bucket.

But just as he made the leap inside, he heard boxes overturn and the bucket roll away behind him. Something caught him by the tail. Dragged out in reverse, he found himself looking into the upside-down face of a cat.

Ricky wiggled and clawed at her grip, even knowing that his chance to escape was slim.

Some superheroes they were. Four of them against one half-starved mouse. He wouldn't talk though. No matter how hungry he was. Even if they tortured him.

=^.,.^=

Chapter Twenty-Two

FREDDY SKIRTED THE rusty bucket, hopped through the mouse hole, and emerged again with a frayed backpack. Freddy slipped his thin arms through the loops and half dragged, half carried it back.

Everyone watched the mouse dangle from Catt's paw.

"Let me go!" Ricky squealed. The ground didn't look so far away, if he could wriggle loose from Catt's grip.

But she held on tight. She didn't want to hurt the mouse, but he was going to answer some questions before she let go.

Patty felt something bump against her leg. She lifted the backpack off Freddy's shoulders. "Well, well, well…" she said, digging through the pack.

She grimaced at a moldy cheese sandwich and tossed it into the dumpster. Ricky tried to catch it, but Catt brought him closer to her face and scowled. A thread-bare blanket came next and, then, a shiny gold phone.

Patty dropped the backpack. Her focus was the phone.

"You must have stolen this," she said.

"Did not!" Ricky said. "I found it fair and square. And I'm not telling you my passcode."

Brows pulled down, Patty tapped on the screen. After a few tries, she held up the lit screen, proudly labeled "Ricky's Phone," pumping her hoof in the air.

"'Cheese.' Not a very original password, Ricky," she sneered.

● ● ●

"Catt," Simon said with concern. "We mice don't like hanging upside down. All the blood rushes to the head. Can you put him down without letting him go?"

Catt set the mouse down, pinning his tail with her back paw. She cupped her front paws around his body, allowing him enough freedom to move but not escape. When she looked up, Simon, Patty, and Freddy were staring at the phone, while Patty scrolled through the photo gallery.

"Yup," she said. "He followed Catt all day. From Mrs. Gee's house to Mouseville and back, all over town to here. Plus, there are some from today."

Patty faced Ricky. She loved movies, and tough guys in movies always squinted and talked in low voices when interrogating prisoners. Not that Ricky was a prisoner. But he was a suspect with information. Investigators in the movies held suspects and questioned them for information. Some got pretty mean when they needed answers.

Patty could be mean too. Well…maybe.

● ● ●

Ricky pushed against Catt's paws. He wouldn't cower like a lowly rat, despite the pig's interrogation. He hadn't done anything.

He hated that the Simons in the world got every break. While his friends and family worked themselves nearly to death, they still starved. Simon had a safe, cozy village to go home to. Well, not anymore. But Ricky had never had a home. Simon's family didn't starve or huddle behind dumpsters to stay warm. No, Simon had a snug bed and so much food, they threw the leftovers away! Ricky wasn't proud to admit he used to walk all the way to Mouseville at least twice a week just for their garbage. It tasted better than what he ate most days.

That happened to be where he was going just yesterday—the Mouseville garbage dump. As he had scampered down the road, he considered Mouseville and its uppity citizens.

Especially Simon. So important. So busy finding treasure, he couldn't waste time talking to Ricky. Because Ricky was City. Simon was Country. He had no time to help Ricky's family make their lives better.

In fact, Simon wasn't the clever hero everyone thought he was. Ricky knew better. Why, he chose a cat for a best friend! Then he'd taken her to Mouseville, where Ricky wasn't welcome. That had been the last straw.

Ricky had been so angry, kicking rocks and stomping down the road to Mouseville, that he hadn't noticed the snake until he was trapped. Just his luck too. Ricky curled his paws over his head and waited for the fangs to pierce his skin. But one flick from the snake's tongue snapped Ricky into action.

What would Simon do? Simon always talked his way out of these predicaments. He would have gotten the snake to consider a trade. That's it, a trade! But what for?

Ricky had only thought of his own life when he traded it for a way into Mouseville. Not his proudest achievement, but he'd thought he was going to die.

At that moment, he had known he was smarter than Simon. He'd made the tough choice. The words slipped easily from his mouth.

Ricky had promised the cold-blooded predator a feast. Fat, happy mice, not ten feet away.

He hid his smile, then led the snake to where the garbage was dumped. The snake slithered through the small opening into Mouseville. Ricky hid under a tree root and waited for the screams.

It was a story he would tell his grandchildren: how he escaped a snake by using his wits.

• • •

Ricky had been so caught up in his dreams, he almost missed Catt leaving Mouseville. She'd run past his hiding spot with the snake's severed head. After burying the snake, she'd sat outside Mouseville for a spell with her ears laid flat. Eventually, she had given up and left, stopping every few feet to look back.

Ricky followed Catt to Mrs. Gristle's house. She had to stop to wipe her eyes and nose, but then she had sprinted. She ran so fast, Ricky had barely kept up. In fact, he had just reached the house, when Catt ran out of it, down the empty street, toward the city. Ricky caught his breath as Simon and Mrs. Gee called and searched for Catt around the house. When they had gone back inside, Ricky left to find her himself.

She had made it all the way to the city. In the alley behind the deli, she'd hiccuped and sniffled until well after the sun set.

During the night, Ricky had watched Catt interact with Melvin. She offered him food, as well as her body for warmth.

Ricky had shivered beneath his worn blanket, his hollow stomach aching. He couldn't sleep but fitfully. No one watched over him. He was always cold, always in danger.

Chapter Twenty-Three

"SO, AFTER I killed the snake, you sent the cats!" Catt screeched, pushing her nose against Ricky's.

He shook his head, panicked. He hadn't meant to tell them anything. "Uh, I didn't see any cats," he said in a quavering voice. "I don't know any cats. The snake was, uh, a mistake. I was scared. When you left, I did too. I mean, I saw some cats at Mrs. Gristle's house, but I never talked to them. I swear!" Ricky held up one paw and covered his heart with the other.

"I think he's telling the truth," Patty said. "Look at these." Patty passed Ricky's phone to Simon, then Catt. "I think we know who tore the village apart."

Catt studied the pictures of her and Simon. Then Patty zoomed in on the background. Buff and Bash, the twin cats from Superhero School, handed mouse-hut pieces to...Nigel! In Mrs. Gee's backyard. Nigel? Catt looked at Simon.

How did the twins know how to get into Mouseville, and what did Nigel have to do with it?

"Simon?" Catt asked. "If the twins ruined Mouseville, then why do the mice think I'm responsible?"

Simon kicked a can. "I don't know, Catt. Grandma said you must have told them the way in. What it comes down to is that you're a cat, and mice do not trust cats. We assume you're all on the same side."

● ● ●

Freddy grabbed the phone. "Nigel?" His eyes swiveled between Catt and Simon. "If Nigel is part of this, I'm afraid Mrs. Gee could be hurt."

Freddy handed Patty the phone, which she packed in her case.

"I wouldn't want to tell her that her right-hand man is involved. But Nigel can't be trusted. Not until we know exactly what's going on."

Patty reached for Catt's paw. "I'm sorry, but we need to go somewhere safe until we figure this out."

"Mrs. Gee's?" Catt asked.

Simon stopped pacing just long enough to say, "Not Mrs. Gee's. Nigel is there."

"Follow us," Patty said.

Catt wrapped Ricky in one paw and Melvin in the other, worrying over Mrs. Gee as she slinked down the road to Mr. Miller's farm.

● ● ●

Inside Patty's barn, Simon and Patty settled into chairs on either side of the desk. Patty typed on her laptop, while Simon scribbled on a notepad.

Freddy hopped about, fetching drinks, pens, and paper. He offered Catt a clean blanket and pillow for the sleeping, sniffling Melvin. He tied two storage crates together to hold Ricky, but not before furnishing the pen with a blanket, pillow, and dish of peanuts.

Freddy was obviously comfortable here. Shuffling through drawers and cabinets, he never asked where anything was kept. Catt knew a friendship existed between Patty and Freddy, but now she saw more.

Freddy squatted beside Patty, waiting to serve. As though reading her mind, he was always ready with whatever she needed. Humming a happy tune, he chopped fruits and vegetables in the kitchen and arranged a snack platter, along with cheese and crackers. Freddy filled and set a small plate beside Patty, then handed another to Catt. After everyone was served, Freddy resumed his spot next to Patty's chair.

Everyone was working, but Catt didn't know what to do. She wasn't clever like Simon, or smart like Patty, or helpful like Freddy. She tried to think of something useful she could do, but she fell asleep instead.

When a flapping noise startled her awake, she sat up, rubbed her eyes, and blinked.

Simon clapped again as a sly smile stretched across his face.

"We're going to convince Nigel to throw Mrs. Gee a surprise party," he said. "That'll keep Nigel busy and give us a reason to take Mrs. Gee out of the house without tipping him off."

Simon pointed at the picture on Patty's desk. It was from Ricky's phone. When did they do that? Catt licked her paw and rubbed it over her cheek, while Patty and Simon argued over details.

● ● ●

"And why would Nigel go along with this?" Patty asked. "I mean, you can't just throw a random surprise party. It's not her birthday."

She banged her way around the desk to look at the picture with Simon. "What I don't get is why Nigel would do all this. Now? With Catt living in the house, it's the worst time for shenanigans."

"She-what-agains?" Catt asked, spitting out hair.

"Crazy plans," Patty said. "Why would he risk everything to tear up a mouse nest? No offense, Simon."

She frowned, reading from Simon's notepad. "You think he's evil?" She laughed. "Nigel? That's crazy!"

Simon said, "I think Catt is what changed." He held up a paw when Patty tried to interrupt. "Think about it. Catt lives with Mrs. Gee too. If," he drew out the word, "Nigel did anything strange, Catt would notice. She pays attention, even when she doesn't realize she's doing it."

Simon sat and folded his arms behind his head. "She might already know something. Can you think of a faster way to get her out then to brand her a criminal? Without any proof, who would you believe? Nigel, who is an upstanding and well-known member of Sweet Meadows, or Catt, who is a new stray from someplace called Cal-I-FORN-ia?" He pronounced Catt's previous address like a foreign word.

"Exactly. Nigel doesn't know Ricky took pictures of him, or else he'd be out looking for him." Simon banged his fist on the desk. "But he's not. He's home, acting like everything's the same."

Chapter Twenty-Four

NIGEL CARRIED A large bowl of milk onto the back porch—a treat for his underlings. The Siamese cats lunged at it before he could set it down.

The butler clicked his tongue at their bad manners. Manners were important to Nigel, whose job depended on proper behavior.

Though Nigel hated working with such despicable creatures, he needed brawn without brains, as well as someone to take the fall, should it come to that. The two buffoons were easy enough to convince—willing to do anything for money. But he wished they didn't require so much guidance. He had to direct their every step, as they were unable to think for themselves. Bullies without sense or morals.

They were just the means to an end. See, Nigel was done serving others. All his hard work had paid off and it was time to quit.

Working for Mrs. Gristle presented extra opportunities he was quick to take advantage of. Nigel was in charge of all the Gristles' fortune. He had a knack for investment, and Mrs. Gristle boasted to her neighbors. If Nigel could make so much money for her, he could make money for them too. Her friends admired Nigel's loyalty to Mrs. Gristle after Mr. Gristle died, and they also trusted him with their banking.

Currently, Nigel controlled most of the money in Sweet Meadows. Not that he needed all that money when his name was on the Gristle accounts. But he funneled little bits at a time into his private bank account in Switzerland, which he'd opened under a false name.

Furthermore, Nigel knew Mrs. Gristle had recently taken a job on the side. When she asked him for her account number so her employer could deposit her paycheck into the bank, he gave her his Swiss account. She didn't know the difference. He was proud of that scam. Knowing Mrs. Gristle worked to build his personal fortune was a bonus. The small salary she insisted on paying him was a joke compared to what he stole from her and her friends.

Mrs. Gristle was quite rich on her own, a fact that Nigel kept under wraps, even from Mrs. Gristle. The bank manager was easily bribed, taking his small cut of the money. Nigel worked tirelessly for ten years, waiting for the day he inherited the estate. And, until two days ago, Nigel was certain that he would.

Every detail was lining up and right on schedule. Until Simon showed up with that sniveling, whiney Catt. They'd convinced his mistress to adopt Catt, making her Mrs. Gristle's only family and first in line to inherit all her money. That was supposed to be Nigel's position. As executor, he would have full access to everything.

But Catt now stood in the way. Years of cooking, cleaning, bowing, and scraping, all the while biting his tongue, erased in the time it took to sign a dotted line.

As of yesterday, Catt was the new heiress. Every penny of the fortune would belong to that sad, flea-ridden mongrel.

Now Nigel needed to get rid of Catt and inherit the estate and fast. The bank manager had fallen ill and taken leave. If anyone noticed Nigel's creative banking, he would be eating prison food.

The plan was simple. Nigel had overheard Simon say he was taking Catt to meet his family. He followed them, undercover, until Simon and Catt disappeared through a wall of vines. Then he called the twins and told them where to go. They would destroy the mouse village. When Catt tried to defend the mice, which she would, the twins would capture her and meet Nigel at the abandoned shack on Mr. Miller's farm.

Once they had Catt kidnapped, Nigel would convince her to leave, or else they would not only destroy Simon's home, but kill his family too. Nigel would force Catt to write a farewell letter, telling Mrs. Gristle to cancel the adoption because she's leaving Sweet Meadows for good.

It would've worked too. If the knuckle-head twins had only paid attention. Instead, they let a stupid snake mess up Nigel's careful plan, while Catt slipped away, colliding with him and his tea tray in Mrs. Gristle's hall. He had smothered his rage then, and now he had to keep the twins happy and quiet while he made another perfect plan.

This time, Nigel would get rid of Catt for good.

Chapter Twenty-Five

IN A CORNER of the barn Patty called home, Catt tucked Melvin in tighter. She hadn't had kittens of her own, but if she ever did, she hoped she'd feel as protective of them as she did this little mouse. She even felt sorry for Ricky and fed him through the slats of his crate.

Simon paced again, thinking. Catt watched him stop, dig through his pockets, mutter something, then resume his back and forth trek around the barn. She counted twenty-three laps so far.

Patty, nose buried in her laptop, dug for information on Nigel. Most of it was ordinary, except for a foreign bank account with a lot of money. Patty figured it was one of Mrs. Gee's accounts with Nigel's name on it. But Simon wasn't buying it. He thought Nigel was up to something and possibly stealing from Mrs. Gee.

When asked where she got this information, Patty wouldn't say. She just winked and started typing again.

Freddy, quiet and efficient, served juice and snacks, refilling empty cups and restocking dishes without a word. He was particularly aware of Patty's needs. When she reached for a soda, he replaced it with bottled water. After the second bowl of chips disappeared, he set the dish of carrot sticks closer to Patty.

When she reached for a pen, Freddy nudged it under her hoof. When she laid her head against the back of her chair, he hopped on it and squeezed drops in her eyes, then slipped her a pair of reading glasses. When Patty sneezed, he whisked her a tissue. She never missed a stroke on her keyboard or took her eyes off the screen. She lifted a hoof, and he handed her whatever she needed. Catt had never known such a fluent friendship.

Freddy obviously admired the pretty pig. If Patty ever stopped working long enough, she would see it too. He took excellent care of her so she could focus on her work. They were partners in the best way.

Catt thought she should be more like Freddy, considering that Simon was more knowledgable. But Catt wasn't a partner at all. Instead of helping Simon clean up the mess, she was the one who made the messes.

Patty collected information, while Freddy took care of her. Simon planned their next steps, while Catt napped.

She should be helping, not waiting. But how? She didn't know computers. She had no idea what anyone wanted or needed. She wasn't good at planning or solving puzzles. What could she do?

Catt always waited to be told what to do, and she was sick of it. She must be good at something. If she could figure out what it was, then she would know how to help.

● ● ●

As the trio worked, Catt tried to pin down what they had missed. They had plenty of questions, but no answers. Maybe she could get some answers for them.

Catt pulled up Melvin's blanket, fed Ricky the rest of her cheese and crackers, then slipped outside. Once she was sure nobody had followed her, she headed to Mrs. Gristle's house. Nigel would be there.

Rain fell, soft and gentle at first, then harder and faster, until it was pelting Catt's head. The shortcut through the field had been a good idea when it was dry. But now, sliding and clawing through the muddy grass, on her back as much as her paws, she was taking twice as long.

When the rain beat down, Catt ran through the open door of a run-down shack, hidden in the trees. The weathered gray boards creaked when she pulled the door closed. The rain pummeled the rusted roof and the wind shook the thin walls, but the inside was warm and dry. And very dark.

When her eyes adjusted to the dimness, she checked out the house. She jumped onto a bed and licked her soggy fur. Catt hated being wet.

When she looked up from grooming, she saw a piece of knotted rope dangling from one of the bedposts. That's odd, she thought.

Following the rope to where it disappeared, Catt crawled under the bed. There, she found rope tied to all four bedposts. She also uncorked a brown bottle that held a sickeningly sweet-smelling liquid. Catt briefly wondered what it was for and who left it here. But then she remembered that Sweet Meadows was different from California and she had seen lots of strange things since she got here.

Catt snuggled into the bed quilt. It was a little scratchy and threadbare, but at least it was warm and clean. Soon she drifted to sleep, imagining Simon's face when she fixed her problems, all by herself.

=^.,.^=

Chapter Twenty-Six

"WELL, WELL, WELL," Nigel slurred, rubbing his pale paws together. His little trap had sprung itself.

Oh, he was a genius. Nigel thought of all the ways to torture a nosy cat, but he stayed still and silent in the shadows of the loft, watching his sleeping prey like an eagle on the hunt. For he was hunting.

This nobody cat had already messed up Nigel's future. He should be lying on a beach by now, attended by waiters eager to respond to a single snap of his fingers. Instead, he was stuck in a musty farm shack, trying not to breathe in the odor of cow pies and horse apples. Cutesy names for disgusting messes do not make them cute or appealing! Makes me sick…

Catt's dash to the shack was too lucky. He couldn't have planned it better himself. Did he control things with his mind? That would be a useful superpower indeed, Nigel thought.

He had slipped out of Mrs. Gristle's house during the rainstorm to remove any evidence linking him to the shack. He was packing up the loft, when Catt scrambled inside. He had watched her find the ropes and sniff the bottle, before curling up on the bed and falling asleep.

Maybe he didn't need a new plan after all.

• • •

Nigel slipped down the staircase and stood over Catt, watching her chest rise and fall. He picked up the brown bottle and smiled. His teeth, yellow and sharp, showed as he poured the smelly liquid onto a rag. Holding his breath and the rag at arm's length, Nigel covered Catt's head with the cloth and pressed it over her nose and mouth.

She jerked awake. Her legs kicked wildly, and she clawed at the rag. But Catt felt suddenly dizzy and too tired to fight. Her paws felt clumsy. The sweet, sickening fumes burned her throat, overpowering her. Her limbs flopped to the bed as she drifted into the dark nothing.

• • •

Nigel watched Catt's body twitch and fall still. The drug worked faster than he'd thought, but that was good. He was strong enough to hold her down, but not for long. Catching her asleep had worked in his favor too. His plans always had a way of working themselves out. He didn't need the twins' muscle. He had a brilliant mind, and he would get everything he deserved.

Nigel considered his choices. If he didn't leave soon, the old hag he worked for would miss him and ask questions. He decided to employ the twins one last time. They could watch Catt while he kept his boss happy. He wouldn't have to serve her much longer.

Nigel made a quick call to Buff and Bash. Then he used his phone to record a message, muffling his voice with his paw:

"I have your beloved Catt. If you ever want to see her again, you must wire $250,000 to this account…" Might as well take advantage of the situation, Nigel snickered to himself.

As he tied Catt's legs to the bed, he congratulated himself for getting rid of another of Mrs. Gristle's strays. He thought alley cats to be idle, bad-mannered, germ-carrying mongrels. Mrs. Gristle was too moved by their sad stories. Still, Nigel wanted to see Mrs. Gristle's face when she learned about her newfound family member. How very disappointing.

"Keep her knocked out and tied up until I come back," he told the twins. He then hurried out the door, whistling along his way home.

Letting everything else go, Nigel focused on the recipe he'd picked for Mrs. Gristle's dinner. Tuna casserole was her favorite and would be perfect tonight.

Chapter Twenty-Seven

FREDDY WAS BEST at two things: listening and following. And he could do both without anyone's notice.

He watched Catt slip out and cut across the fields toward Sweet Meadows. He had no idea where she was going, but he figured he should see her there safely. Not that he could do much in a dangerous situation, but he was quick and nearly invisible. As Patty always said, "You're like the fly on the wall. No one sees it."

When it began raining, Freddy thought Catt would turn back. The wet cat slipped in the mud, while the frog splashed from puddle to puddle. When Catt sprinted up the hill, Freddy scrambled to catch up.

She pulled the shack door shut as he leaped for the opening, but it closed in his face. When Freddy found a small crack in a window, he sneaked inside. The place smelled like a cow, but it looked cleaner than any other abandoned shack he knew of.

A spider scurried away as Freddy's tongue shot out. Darn. He needed a snack. Hopping uphill was exhausting.

Freddy hid in the fireplace, while Catt groomed. He didn't want to embarrass her so he turned his face to the wall. Leaving a puddle on the floorboards, she crawled onto a bed and fell asleep.

Boring. Freddy's special mission was watching Catt sleep? Well, for her sake, he'd keep his eyes open.

Something wasn't right. The shack was too clean. So was that quilt. The floors had been swept recently. There weren't any cobwebs or dust.

Hungry, he inspected the corners for a light meal. But there was not so much as a gnat buzzing around. Nothing looked out of place, which would be impressive, except that it was an old shack. He would expect splintered boards, broken dishes, and moldy old newspapers. Did someone live here?

Mr. Miller never used this house because it was falling down. Yet Freddy saw patches where there were holes in the roof and tape on the windows. Firewood was stacked by the hearth. Mr. Miller talked about tearing the house down, not fixing it up. Then who did this? The old farmer never cleaned this shack, and he wouldn't leave a good building unused either.

Freddy felt fear trickle down his back.

He hopped out of the fireplace to check the other rooms when he heard footsteps in the upstairs loft. He jumped behind the woodpile in time to see two polished black shoes skip down the steps.

The meerkat snatched a bottle from under the bed and stood over Catt. He poured the contents of the bottle onto a rag. Even from across room, Freddy recognized the sweet, chemical smell: chloroform.

Eyes round and watchful, Freddy gaped as Nigel placed the rag over Catt's face. She struggled against his hold, but the chloroform worked within seconds, leaving her powerless.

Catt was in serious danger, and Freddy was trapped.

Nigel made two phone calls, one a chilling request to bring money or else. When Nigel tied Catt's legs to the bed, Freddy inched back through the hole in the window. Hopping as fast as his legs allowed, he hoped Simon and Patty would know how to rescue Catt.

Freddy dove into a patch of poison ivy to avoid Buff and Bash, who were bolting toward the shack. He gratefully gulped down a dragonfly, then carried on his way. He needed sustenance to make it down the hill and not croak.

Nigel came along minutes later, whistling and grinning. As Freddy bounded down the hill to Patty's, he couldn't remember ever seeing the meerkat act anything other than cranky.

Chapter Twenty-Eight

PATTY AND SIMON looked up when Freddy slammed the door.

"Hey, Freddy," Simon said. "Where you been?"

Patty had already turned back to her computer.

"Riiibbbit! Uh, hmm, croooakkk!" Freddy cleared his throat. "Ahem. We've got trouble!" His voice was dry and deep, like rocks inside a bucket.

Patty's hoofs paused midair at Freddy's strange tone. He never raised his voice or exaggerated anything. If he thought it was trouble, it was.

"Out with it! Whatever bug flew down your throat, it can't be worse than this." Patty waved at the files and pictures scattered on every surface.

Simon dismissed Freddy with the flick of a paw and returned to pacing.

Freddy hated talking. But Simon's ignoring him was worse.

"I followed Catt to the old shack up the hill," he said, spacing out his words.

Simon stopped to look around. "Catt left?"

"She got caught in the rain and—"

"It's raining?" Patty peered out the smudged window.

Freddy wiped his brow. Was he the only one who paid attention? "She got caught in the rain, so she fled into the shack. I followed her. It was clean. The shack. Too clean. Not like Mr. Miller at all."

Freddy was getting off track. He needed to stick to the important facts. Facts would help Catt. "I had a bad feeling about it, but Catt fell asleep, then Nigel came down the steps, and—"

"Wait!" Simon said. "Nigel was there?"

Freddy nodded, then screeched, "He knocked Catt out and tied her up and recorded a message asking for $250,000!"

The room fell dead quiet. Freddy never screamed. He never lost his temper. He was always calm. Simon and Patty stared at him as if he'd grown a second head. Then a clap of thunder broke the spell.

Questions rained down on Freddy like the drops pelting the window. He answered them, adding as many details as he remembered.

"He wants ransom money for Catt?" Patty asked.

Simon got in Freddy's face. "Why didn't you help her?"

"I can't fight a meerkat! Not to mention his two stooges. I'm only a frog! We all need to help Catt."

Patty slipped her arm around Freddy's shoulders and glared at Simon until he stepped back.

"At this point, Nigel doesn't know we know he's up to something," she said. "If Freddy had intervened, he would be right next to Catt, tied up and useless. This way we know, and we can try to get her out."

Simon sighed and nodded. "You're right. Aw, I'm sorry, Freddy. I'm just worried about Catt!"

Patty patted Simon's shoulder.

"So are we," said Freddy.

Patty reached for her tablet and stylus, creating a detailed rescue mission with graphs and maps. Simon added a few maneuvers to outsmart the twins.

But they needed to catch Nigel in the act. It was their only hope to clear Catt's name and get justice for Simon's family. Other than Freddy's word, they had nothing on Nigel for either crime, and he could easily throw the twins under the bus and show up with clean hands.

They still didn't know what that crafty butler was up to.

On Ricky's phone, Patty found hundreds of photos of Catt and Simon, including the ones from outside Mrs. Gee's house yesterday morning. She zipped through them, but eventually returned to one.

Patty zoomed in on it. Finally, she looked up with an enormous grin. When Simon and Freddy saw what Patty found, they high-fived and danced a jig.

As the photos progressed, showing Simon and Catt on their way to Mouseville, Patty was able to see Nigel, or a part of Nigel, hidden in almost every scene.

Nigel had followed them! He knew where Mouseville was and he likely informed the twins.

"Why?" Simon asked. "To get Catt arrested? Why would he want to get rid of Catt? The only link between Catt and Nigel is Mrs. Gee, and that's only because Mrs. Gee adopted her. Why would that matter to Nigel? He doesn't act like he likes Catt, but he doesn't act like he likes anyone!"

Patty held up a hoof. "That's it! The adoption!"

"What about it?"

"If Mrs. Gee adopted Catt, then Catt is the heir to the Gristle fortune! If Nigel doesn't like that, then it's because he expected to inherit the estate when Mrs. Gee—you know—takes the trip to cat heaven."

"I wouldn't put it past Nigel to send Mrs. Gee on her way early," Freddy said with a shiver.

"Yes…" The clues wiggled inside Patty's head, like puzzle pieces fitting themselves together. The picture was clearer, but Patty didn't know yet how to use it.

She needed to eat. Patty did her best plotting while eating.

"Operation Rescue Catt at dawn!" Simon crowed.

Chapter Twenty-Nine

CATT WOKE UP with a splitting headache. Her stomach seethed and tried to empty, but nothing came out. She didn't know how long she'd been sleeping, but it was still dark. When she tried to pull her legs up, they wouldn't budge. She pulled harder, but she was tightly bound by each limb to the bed frame.

Her ears twitched. She heard footsteps in another room. She stretched with all her might, but the ropes didn't give. Twisting and turning, she worked to slip free so she could fight whatever was coming.

A lantern bobbed through the inky darkness somewhere in the house, swallowing the shadows in greedy gulps. Catt's mouth felt like it was stuffed with cotton. She licked her lips and gnawed at the rope around her leg. The rope was new and thick. It tasted bitter, and the fibers poked her nose.

The light moved closer. Soft, steady footsteps matched the lantern's swing. Whoever it was wanted her afraid. They were toying with her. Knowing she couldn't escape, they wanted her to squirm anyway.

When the light reached the bedside, Catt blinked at the harsh glare and saw the flash of Buff's cruel grin.

• • •

Or maybe it was Bash… She'd only seen them twice before and hadn't cared enough to tell them apart. They were always together, so it didn't matter anyway.

Had the twins waited for her to come to this shack? How did they know she would be here? She detoured because of the rain, which was by chance, so how did they find her? Catt didn't have long to wonder.

The twin cat cackled. His lips curled over yellow teeth. He looked like the opossums who teased Catt during those first terrifying nights on the streets.

"Hey, Bash! The captive's awake," he called over his shoulder.

Buff pressed his nose against Catt's. His rotten breath made her gag and spit sprayed her face. "Not so smug now, are you? No little mouse friend to get you out of this jam."

He flicked one ear and then the other. Buff straightened and held the lantern high, making him look taller…and scarier. "The mouse will learn who runs this town and that you don't have any place in it."

His words hit her like garbage dumped over her head. Catt cringed at the awful smell. When she closed her eyes, he leaned in.

"No one knows you're here. No one's coming to help. Because you're nothing."

Buff let the terrible truth hang in the air, along with the stench of his breath. Then he turned and took the lantern— the only light in the house—with him.

Catt felt the dark smother her, like that oily rag had. Goosebumps traveled under her fur, making it stand on end. She wondered if Simon had noticed she was gone yet. She'd really messed up this time. Even Simon's best tricks couldn't get her out of here.

The lantern came close again. She tensed, afraid of what would happen next. She prayed that they brought food. Her growling stomach made its discomfort known.

When the light reached her bed, the same sweet odor as before overwhelmed her. Catt twisted her head to avoid the rag, but it found her mouth and nose anyway, and she felt her body sliding into the black, bottomless pit of restless sleep.

● ● ●

Bash watched Buff press the dirty rag in Catt's face. Her whole body shook at first, but the poison's effect was rapid. Her body relaxed, her limbs lay limp on the bed, and she slept.

Bash hates this part of his twin—the brutal, do-whatever-it-takes-to-get-on-top side. Bash never set out to be a bully, but it happened by following Buff's lead. Buff wouldn't know a good idea if it hit him in the nose.

But Bash knew this was a bad idea.

He didn't trust Nigel. The meerkat was only in this for himself. He wouldn't take care of them. They were his puppets—there to do Nigel's dirty work and take the fall for him afterward. Bash told Buff that, but he refused to listen to reason.

Buff was stubborn, particularly when he thought he was being made a fool. He never learned to read or write, so Bash had always covered for him. Being identical, Bash took tests for his twin and completed all his school assignments, as well.

He didn't want to abandon his brother, but it was getting harder to go along with Buff's crazy plans. He shook his head at the tied and sleeping Catt. Buff had gone too far.

Bash stood guard over Catt in the dark. She looked peaceful, if not for the ropes. He couldn't leave her like that. Bash reached into his boot, pulled out his knife, and sliced through the ties. Bash crossed Catt's front paws over her chest. She would sleep for a few hours.

● ● ●

Buff sat at the table in the kitchen, sharpening his claws. Bash dropped into a chair and leaned back to rest his boots on the table. He hoped that some sleep would erase all the bad feelings before Buff woke him for the second shift.

Unable to doze off, he worried that Buff would find Catt untied and do something worse to her.

"Buff," he said. "I'll take the first watch. You get some shut eye. I'll wake you in a couple hours."

"Now you're talking, brother," Buff yawned.

He curled himself into a ball, and soon his snores rattled the drab walls of the shack.

But Bash wouldn't wake Buff up tonight. He would keep watch all night and let Catt sleep, unharmed and unbound.

● ● ●

Bash jerked awake to a noise from the back of the house. He hadn't meant to fall asleep, but it was almost daylight. A quick glance at Buff, still curled up and snoring, and his tense muscles unknotted. He had closed his eyes again when he heard a slight creak.

Bash's eyes popped open to see Catt, tiptoeing down the hall. He closed his eyes and pretended to sleep until she reached the front door.

Bash snorted and let his thick boots fall to the floor, to cover the noise of Catt opening the door. Buff rolled over but didn't wake up.

Catt held her breath and waited. Bash watched under his lashes as she stood in the doorway, silhouetted by the sunrise. Then she slipped away.

Bash smiled, shifted to a more comfortable position, and let his dreams take over.

Chapter Thirty

CATT HURRIED ACROSS the wet grass, barely able to catch her breath for fear that Buff or Bash would drag her back. She slipped and slid down the hill. The storm from the night before left an eerie fog on the ground.

The sun was beginning to peek over Mr. Miller's farmhouse. Catt raced over ruts and rocks, toward her friends and safety. She wanted to scream as loud as she could to wake them.

While sneaking out of the shack, Catt had considered her next steps. She'd listened for any noise to indicate that the twins were awake. What would Simon do? The question repeated with every careful step.

Simon couldn't always be with her. Catt needed to take care of herself. She should be more like her mouse friend, who always had a plan. Simon was honest. He stood up for himself and others. He didn't run away from his problems, like Catt did. He met them head-on, sorting through challenges until the situation changed. Simon had courage—more than anyone she'd ever met.

But she wasn't Simon. Catt didn't know how to put things right. She didn't know how to settle the misunderstanding between her and the mice of Mouseville. On top of everything else, the twins were out to get her, and Nigel was somehow involved. How could she avoid danger and make everyone believe her?

Catt felt helpless. She needed help, but she also needed to help herself.

She heard a siren blare and fade in the distance. The police… They were probably out looking for the cat who destroyed Mouseville.

Maybe that was her only hope. If she turned herself in, the police would investigate and find her innocent. Then all of Sweet Meadows would know she was neither a criminal nor a traitor.

Without any proof, would they believe her?

It was a risk, but she would do it to make Simon proud. He believed in her, when no one else did.

● ● ●

Catt changed her destination to the Sweet Meadows Police Department. Her heart beat so hard inside her ribs, she barely heard the officer's tired "Howdy" as she approached the front desk.

"Can I help you, miss?" A droopy-eyed basset hound in a police cap didn't look up from his newspaper.

"I, um—" Catt wet her lips. There would be no going back from here. She must face the consequences, whatever they might be. "I'm Catt. I'm here about the Mouseville incident."

The dog dropped the paper, his sagging eyelids popping open. "Uh, just a moment please."

He picked up a phone and spoke slowly into the receiver. "This is Officer Max. Catt the cat is here to turn herself in."

He whispered behind his paw, "You know, the suspect..."
Catt shrunk away. "Uh-huh. Okay. Uh-huh..."

When he hung up, he pointed drowsy eyes at Catt.
"Sergeant Jones can take your confession—uh, I mean, your
report. Please take a seat over there."

● ● ●

Catt waited on a hard, plastic chair in the hall. She'd never
been inside a police station before. The station was clean
and quiet, with sparse plastic or metal furniture and thick,
bulletproof windows. She imagined this was how a goldfish
felt—exposed.

Catt felt the walls caving in. Tears burned the backs of
her eyes, but she refused to cry. She would do this with grace
and courage.

A minute later, a buzzer released the lock on the door
in the hall. A tall giraffe in blue uniform ducked under the
doorway and waved his hoof at Catt.

She pictured Simon beside her, smiling and joking. If her
best friend were here, she wouldn't be so afraid. Just thinking
about him calmed her. She squared her shoulders, like she'd
seen Simon do, rose onto her toes, and strode into the room.

When the door closed behind her with a loud click, Catt
knew her life would forever be divided into before and after:
before her trip to Mouseville, and after she killed that snake.

● ● ●

"Please have a seat." The sergeant pulled out a chair for Catt,
taking one opposite the table for himself. His long legs occu-
pied most of the space under the table.

He opened a brown folder and read aloud. With each
crime and accusation, Catt's confidence slipped a little more.

When he offered her a lawyer—whatever that was—Catt laid her head on the table and closed her eyes.

"Catt the cat, you are under arrest," Sergeant Jones said, but not unkindly.

Before the police could ask any questions or take a statement, she had to sign a paper. The pen felt more awkward than when she'd held one for the first time at Superhero School, but she managed to scratch her name on the line.

The sergeant asked her to stand with her paws behind her back. As the cold handcuffs tightened, she felt her dignity slip away. The officers didn't say anything more but led her through the station, taking her pictures, her prints, her clothes, and her freedom.

Catt sat on a hard cot in a jail cell, picking through a scant meal as she waited. The thin mattress reminded her of how the day had begun. She felt just as scared locked in this jail as she had tied up in the shack.

Chapter Thirty-One

THE PHONE RANG before Operation Rescue Catt got off the ground. The subject of their mission was being held at the Sweet Meadows Police Department, where she'd turned herself in.

Simon listened, his mouth hanging open, while Mrs. Gee relayed the call from the police this morning. Mrs. Gee wanted answers, but Simon, for once, had nothing to say.

After several minutes of arguing, Simon let the phone slide from his ear to the floor. Mrs. Gee scolded him for letting Catt go to the police station alone. No matter how many times he said he didn't know she was going to do that, Mrs. Gee still blamed Simon. Now he knew how Catt felt.

He needed to see Catt, but Mrs. Gee's lawyer said that impossible. Catt had been arrested and no visitation was allowed.

A headache brewed behind his eyes as he tried to make sense of this. Yesterday Catt had been a hostage, and today she was a prisoner. How had she gotten away from Nigel? Some kind of superhero friends they turned out to be. While they slept, Catt had escaped by herself.

No more plans! It was time to act. Simon held his notebook with the rescue mission scribbled on it. He ripped off the page, wadded it into a ball, and crushed it between his paws.

They needed proof to take to the police. They didn't have much, but it would have to be enough. Simon listed every piece of evidence in his notebook:

1. Pictures from Ricky's phone—Nigel following Simon and Catt to Mouseville and Buff and Bash handing pieces of mouse huts to Nigel

Simon had threatened that slimy city mouse within an inch of his life until he finally agreed to give a statement. In it, Ricky admitted that he followed Catt all day and never saw her meet with Nigel or the twins.

2. Ricky's statement
3. Freddy, witness to Catt's kidnapping and Nigel's ransom demand

They needed the message that Freddy overheard Nigel record. Simon kept checking with Mrs. Gee to see if she'd gotten any calls about Catt, but she said no. Did Nigel know Freddy had been hiding in the shack? Had he decided not to demand a ransom after all? Did he know that his hostage was gone? And how did Catt get away from the two biggest, burliest cats in Sweet Meadows by herself? Something smelled rotten.

● ● ●

Simon underlined "RANSOM" several times before letting the pen drop. He slouched in his chair. They were worse off than yesterday.

He smashed a fist in his paw. "We need to stop Nigel!"

"Don't we need free Catt first?" Patty asked. "She's probably terrified!"

"At least she's safe. According to Freddy, Mrs. Gristle may be in danger."

"Simon, Nigel can't do anything until Catt is no longer Mrs. Gee's heir. Let's think this through. By now he knows that Catt isn't tied up in the shack. What would Nigel do next?"

Simon held up a finger. "He'd find a way to make Mrs. Gee reverse the adoption."

"I think you're right. Their next move will be to the lawyer's office. If that's so, then we have a little time to go to the police with our evidence and get Catt released. Then, together, we can stop Nigel before he tries to hurt Mrs. Gee."

Simon thought about what could go wrong. Their plan left a lot to chance, but they were out of time.

Patty took the briefcase from Freddy. "It'll have to do, Simon." She rested her hoof on Simon's shoulder, then opened the door. "C'mon, boys. It's about time we go save Catt."

Chapter Thirty-Two

PATTY DRAGGED FREDDY and Simon behind the bushes in front of the Sweet Meadows Police Department.

"Why are we hiding in the bushes?" Simon snapped.

"Shhh," Patty said. "Look!"

Simon stuck his head out and stared down the sidewalk. He ducked back in time as Nigel led Mrs. Gristle toward the entrance of the police station.

"They're not going to the lawyer. They're going to the police station!"

Simon strained to hear what Nigel was saying but only caught a few phrases: "...shouldn't blame yourself...just a stray...don't know anything...a con artist..."

With every swipe at Catt, Simon felt his ears burn. He kept his paws clenched at his sides to keep from jumping the hedge and wrapping them around Nigel's skinny, lying neck. Nigel tried to convince Mrs. Gee to leave Catt and let the police sort it out.

"Madam," he said, his voice soft and wheedling, "I know you've got the kindest heart, and creatures like Catt take advantage of that." He squeezed her paw between his, holding her back. "Just consider the possibility that it's true. Think of the town's safety. She can be violent and unpredictable. Is she worth putting us all in danger?"

"Nonsense, Nigel. Catt is not that creature. And she is certainly not dangerous." Mrs. Gee pulled her paw free and climbed the steps to the station. Nigel stayed on her heels, pleading with her to see reason.

"Let's go to the lawyer's, madam. The papers are drawn up and waiting to be signed. You must remove that criminal from your noble family lines."

Simon worried that Mrs. Gee would break under the pressure from Nigel and the police. She looked determined, but one or the other might convince her that Catt was a threat.

He wanted to believe that Catt—and Mouseville—would see justice served. He'd always believed in good triumphing over bad. The heroes always save the day and the criminals go to jail. But now he wasn't so sure.

Catt could be locked away forever, or even banished from Sweet Meadows, if Nigel got his way. They had photographs and eye-witness accounts, but would that be enough?

• • •

Patty pulled Simon back behind the hedge. "Everything feels impossible before the third act," she whispered.

Simon nodded. He was too upset to speak and too afraid to think. Not a single idea to save Catt came to mind.

He shoved his paws deep into his pockets, playing with the pieces inside. It was his fault Catt was in jail. If he hadn't insisted she go to Mouseville. If he had not insisted on some crazy, fly-by-the-seat-of-his-pants scheme, Catt could be home cat-napping.

"We have to do something," Simon grunted as he stomped in a tight circle. "We don't know what they're saying in there."

Patty opened the briefcase and pulled out her laptop and cables. She connected them to a bowl-shaped object. Freddy grabbed the bowl, climbed a light pole, and attached it to the window of the station, before hopping down.

Simon frowned as Patty handed him a set of headphones.

Patty fixed her own set over her ears and typed on her laptop. A loud screech, then voices blared through the headphones. That bowl was picking up the sounds inside the station.

"Wow!" Simon exclaimed. With Patty's technology skills and Freddy's detective skills, they just might save the day.

Patty touched a hoof to her lips and pointed at her ear.

Freddy adjusted the volume and donned his own set of headphones.

They listened to the officer explaining the charges against Catt. Then Nigel spoke.

"I don't know why the twins would say I had anything to do with this. Catt probably told them to. I'm sure she must be jealous of my close relationship with Mrs. Gristle. She wants me out of the way, obviously. She's not from here, you know. I worried when Mrs. Gristle agreed to take her in, and I blame myself for not speaking up. Now look where we are."

Simon could hear Mrs. Gee weeping in the background.

"Oh, madam, please don't be upset. This is not good for you." Simon imagined Nigel offering his handkerchief.

An officer's voice broke past the sobbing. "Catt does make a good point. She had no reason to attack Mouseville. She was already inside. Why not do it then? Why involve other cats?"

Nigel sniffed. "Clearly she wanted to fit in here. She thought the cats would like her better if she gave them access to Mouseville. She wouldn't get blamed that way too."

Simon heard papers shuffle, then the officer spoke again. "It's a formality, you understand, but… Mr. Snider, can you tell us where you were when the attack happened? And yesterday afternoon, as well?"

Simon almost cheered aloud, but he didn't want to miss Nigel's answer. A chair scraped the floor before the butler spoke again. "I was home on both days."

Mrs. Gee mumbled something, but Simon couldn't make out what she said. The officer asked, "Did you have something to add, ma'am?"

"I, um, think Nigel forgot that he was gone for a little while both days." Mrs. Gee sounded unlike herself—scared and unsure. What had they said to her before Patty hooked up the audio?

Nigel's velvet voice boomed. "You're confusing your days, madam." To the officer, he said softer, "She's forgetful and easily bewildered."

"No, I'm sure," Mrs. Gristle said, her voice firmer. "You forgot the tea cakes and smoked salmon for brunch. I said it was fine, but you insisted. You were gone a long time."

"That was last week, madam," Nigel said in a cold tone.

"And yesterday? Mrs. Gristle, what do you remember?" the officer asked gently.

"I called him a few times, but he never responded."

"Madam," Nigel whined, "I was in the kitchen. I made your favorite tuna casserole for dinner. It takes all day. You know that. You're very tired." Nigel paused, and a chair creaked. "We should go."

"Just one more question, please," the officer said. "Do you know Buff and Bash Reynolds?"

Mrs. Gristle and Nigel answered at the same time.

"Yes."

"No."

Nigel cleared his throat. "That is, of course, we know who they are, but we don't have contact with them."

Patty flipped the photo out from her cape: Nigel on Mrs. Gee's back porch with Buff and Bash.

Patty waved it. "Gotcha!"

=^.,.^=

172

Chapter Thirty-Three

FREDDY NUDGED SIMON, pointing to the doors when Mrs. Gee exited the building, followed by Nigel. Nigel scurried down the steps, bowing his head to hide a grin. He took Mrs. Gristle's arm and led her down the sidewalk toward the lawyer's office.

Simon's legs felt like jello, and he sat down hard. What did Nigel do? If he could override Mrs. Gee's testimony like that, no one would listen to some kids from Superhero School.

"Wait!" Patty exclaimed. "I have an idea. But I have to hurry. Freddy, help me."

● ● ●

Sergeant Jones reviewed his notes at his desk. Someone was lying, but he didn't know who. Figuring out why someone lies is the best way to solve a mystery. If he could determine a motive, then he could tell who was lying.

He also needed to figure out how the twin cats fit in...

He'd sent two officers to check out the shack, but they immediately called the fire department. On their arrival, the shack was in flames. The police found Buff and Bash, wanted suspects, trudging through the woods with gas cans.

Was this the lucky break Jones needed? Perhaps. It was past time to get some answers.

● ● ●

Across the hall, Catt sat in another room, chained to the table by her leg. She'd had lots of time to think about how to prove her innocence, but she still had no clue. What would Simon do? she wondered. She knew he would face this challenge like any other. Simon could prove he was set up before lunch.

But Catt didn't have any proof. She only had words—her story to tell. It felt strange because, until a few days ago, Catt hadn't used words. Now, words had the power to change her life. So far, using words had gotten her thrown in jail. She wondered if using words could get her free.

● ● ●

The door squeaked, pulling Catt from her regrets.

The giraffe who had handcuffed her yesterday ducked into the small room. When Catt shifted, her chain rattled the table legs.

"Can I get you anything?" Sergeant Jones asked, pointing at the empty cans littering the table—the only things in the room not bolted to the floor.

Catt leaned away from the tall officer and whispered, "No, thanks." Catt made herself sit up straight. She looked the sergeant in the eye when she noticed his shoulders slumped, his sleeves pushed up, and his hair stood up in spikes. Catt felt sorry for him. He's just trying to do his job, she thought, not make my life hard.

When the giraffe looked away from her, she knew. He didn't believe her.

A surge of fear shook her spine. She wasn't getting out of here. Hot tears dripped off her chin to plop on the metal tabletop.

The hard knot in Catt's stomach doubled when the sergeant dropped his hoofs to the table. He pulled a folded handkerchief from his back pocket and slid it toward Catt. Next to it, he laid a candy bar.

Catt's eyes locked on the candy, ignoring the handkerchief until he pushed it closer. She wiped her eyes but never took them off the chocolate.

Sergeant Jones snatched the candy from the table and leaned back in his chair. Slowly, he peeled the wrapper from one corner, breaking off a small piece and holding it out to Catt.

She licked her lips, watching the chocolate melt a little in his hoof before she reached for the treat. The chain stopped her paw short of the chocolate. Her chin trembled, but the giraffe leaned forward and set the candy in her paw. Catt shoved it into her mouth.

For several minutes, they took turns eating bites of chocolate. When it was gone, the officer crumpled the empty wrapper and tossed it on the table. Balancing on the back two legs of the chair, with his hoofs behind his head, he looked at her.

"All right, Catt," he said. "Let's talk."

● ● ●

Catt laid her head on the cool table, detailing every moment until her arrest. Simon and Mouseville. The snake. Running to Mrs. Gristle's house. Sleeping in the alley. Simon, Patty, and Freddy. The rain and the shack. Buff and Bash. Her escape. Then the police station.

Hours passed while Sergeant Jones and Catt explored every fact. Even her voice was exhausted by the end of it.

The officer scratched on his notepad while she talked, asking question after question.

Finally, he dropped his pen on the table. "So you never saw Nigel at Mouseville or the shack?"

Catt raised her chin while she thought about it. "Nigel? No."

Had Nigel been set up too? Ricky had a picture of Nigel and the twins, but maybe it wasn't what it looked like. Maybe Simon had jumped to conclusions.

Catt looked straight at Sergeant Jones and said, "No, I didn't see Nigel." She laid her head back down as all hope disappeared.

The giraffe stood and pulled at his hair. "Without witnesses or proof, my hands are tied. I can't let you go. I'm sorry."

He turned to the door but stopped short. "The twins burned down the shack. They're in jail too, but they're blaming Nigel."

Chapter Thirty-Four

FREDDY CLAPPED HIS hands over Simon's mouth as he blustered.

Catt had given up. Simon heard it in her voice when she answered the sergeant's questions. She didn't know her friends had witnesses and proof of her innocence. They needed to talk to the police now!

Patty snapped the laptop closed, gathered the headphones, and stowed the equipment back in her briefcase while Simon squirmed and squealed.

"Shhh, Simon! Do you want to get us arrested for spying? That won't help her!"

When Patty gave the go-ahead, Freddy released Simon. "He's right, Patty. We've waited long enough."

Patty checked her cape. "Where's my phone?"

Freddy unclipped the phone from her belt and held it up to her.

She switched the audio to speaker phone and waggled her brows. "Listen to this." A crackly recording played: "I have your beloved Catt. If you ever want to see her again, you must wire $250,000 to this account…"

"You hacked into Nigel's phone!" Simon shouted.

"Cool trick, huh?" Patty grinned.

"Guys," Freddy croaked.

But Simon moved closer to Patty as she replayed the message.

"GUYS!" Freddy shrieked, jumping first on Simon's head, then Patty's shoulder.

"WHAT?" Patty and Simon yelled in unison.

He pointed toward the police station. "Play the message for them! We don't have much time before Mrs. Gee signs those papers and Nigel does something awful." He dropped to the ground and bounced up the steps.

Patty clipped her phone back on her belt, picked up the briefcase, and followed Freddy inside.

Simon raced after them and leaped onto the command desk. "We need to see Sergeant Jones right away," he said to the basset hound, who got on his receiver.

● ● ●

Sergeant Jones sauntered into the waiting room. Catt's friends had finally showed up.

This case was full of holes and empty of proof. He doubted this motley crew had any useful information for him, but a good detective must follow every lead. He only had to take care of this interview. Then he could go home, microwave a frozen dinner, and watch basketball.

This day couldn't end soon enough.

● ● ●

Simon jumped up when Sergeant Jones introduced himself. He showed them into a small room, where everyone was seated. The sergeant opened a worn folder on the table.

Simon braced his paws on the table between them. "We know Catt is innocent. We have proof."

Jones fished a notepad and pen from his shirt pocket. "What do you know?"

Patty opened her laptop. After a few clicks, Ricky's pictures appeared. The officer raised his brows and asked Patty to zoom in. Then she pulled out her phone and played the ransom demand.

"That voice sounds familiar," Jones said.

● ● ●

Simon, Patty, and Freddy answered his questions. Patty reluctantly surrendered her phone, and it was bagged, tagged, and whisked away. Another officer brought them sodas.

Annoyed about her phone, Patty found a game to play on her laptop, while Freddy pointed out potential moves. They invited Simon to play, but he declined.

All he could do was pace. Once with his paws behind his back. Then with his arms folded across his chest.

He draped his coat over his left arm, then his right. He took items from his left pocket and put them in his right pocket, then reversed the process. He pulled on his left ear, then his right. He stalked in a circle to the left, then to the right.

His mind buzzed. What if Catt is sent to prison? What if she isn't? Where will I live? Can Mouseville be rebuilt? Is Grandma Whisker still mad? What happened to Joe? Chubby?

He had been so focused on Catt, Simon completely forgot his family and community. Mouseville was still his home, even if he couldn't live there. He hoped that wouldn't be the case after today.

Then Sergeant Jones came back.

"I'm sorry this has taken so long, but I needed a new statement from Buff and Bash." He set a new folder on the table and flipped it open.

"We've arrested Nigel." He stared directly at Simon. "And Catt is free to go."

The trio jumped up, laughing and high-fiving all the way to the front desk, where Catt waited for her hug from Simon.

Chapter Thirty-Five

NIGEL LOOKED SAD and dirty when he shuffled into the courtroom in chains. His usual black livery was replaced with an orange jumpsuit that sagged around his waist. Used to keeping his nose in the air, today, Nigel's eyes locked on the floor in front of him.

Catt and Simon listened to the court officer read the list of Nigel's crimes. A lawyer presented evidence that included years of suspicious bank transactions. The judge struck her gavel hard enough that Catt jumped in her seat.

The discussion between lawyers and judge broke off when Mrs. Gee approached the judge's bench. She spoke quietly, something about "punishment that fits the crime" and "under my supervision."

The judge nodded and banged her gavel again. "Court adjourned!"

A bailiff led Nigel away, his ten years of scheming spoiled in under ten minutes.

● ● ●

Simon leaned against the fourth hut built that day in Mouseville. It was a hot afternoon, but he saw so many changes already.

Nigel balanced on his heels, nails clenched between his teeth. By sundown, he would have two more huts finished. The materials for six more waited in stacks nearby. Nigel's work for tomorrow.

Mrs. Gee, Patty, and Grandma Whisker waved fans to cool the tent where they sat watching the progress. Simon stayed far away from that tent. Since the first day of reconstruction, when they pulled him into yet another argument, Simon had kept his distance. All the mice contributed their ideas, of course, but those three were crazy.

Grandma Whisker wanted everything the way it had always been. Mrs. Gee thought jingly bells and frilly ribbons would be the ideal decoration. While Patty wanted to install "smart" features, so the homeowners could use their cell phones to control lighting and temperature. None of them hesitated to share their crazy ideas with anyone who strayed within earshot.

A brand-new, state-of-the-art security system protected the village. It was the first project completed, along with the new brick wall and electronic gate. Buff and Bash had carried in bricks, boards, and paint every morning. But today, they displayed some skill with the electric saw and drill.

Of course, Buff was useless without Bash. He couldn't read the directions. He was clumsy too. When the twins had been busy bullying, Buff had done all the talking while Bash did all the actual work. No one had noticed before how lazy Buff was. But after their day in court, they both toiled every day, rebuilding Mouseville alongside Nigel. That was Mrs. Gee's idea of justice—making them rebuild what they destroyed, only bigger and better.

Bash didn't seem to mind. He even offered to help with the greenhouse the residents wanted. He drew up plans that included a well and storage.

In a nearby hut, Ricky Rent and little Melvin bickered over the games Simon had brought them. Catt laughed, separating the two with her paw when they started shoving.

"Cut it out, you two," she said. "You don't have to fight for anything anymore. There's plenty to go around."

Mrs. Gee and Catt would dine in Mouseville this night before going home to the yellow house, but no one worried that Catt the cat would hurt anybody.

● ● ●

Simon, Patty, Freddy, and Catt received official letters from the school instructor. Simon kept his letter in one of his pockets at all times, except when he took it out to reread it.

Dear Simon,

    This was your first week of Superhero School, and I must say how impressed I am by what you've learned.

    First, you met a new friend, who was different from you and from a different place. And yet you looked past her differences to become her friend. You gave her a home and a family when she was lacking.

    Then, when that friend was in trouble, you did not abandon her. Nor did you give up in the face of adversity but triumphed over it. Because of you and your friends, justice and truth prevailed in Sweet Meadows. The townsfolk are very grateful.

    You, Simon, are a true hero, with virtues that even the best instructor cannot teach in a classroom.

    And yet, there is still much to learn.

See you in class,
Your Super Mystery Instructor

Official heroes-in-training, Simon, Catt, Patty, and Freddy couldn't wait for their next adventure.

● ● ●

The end.

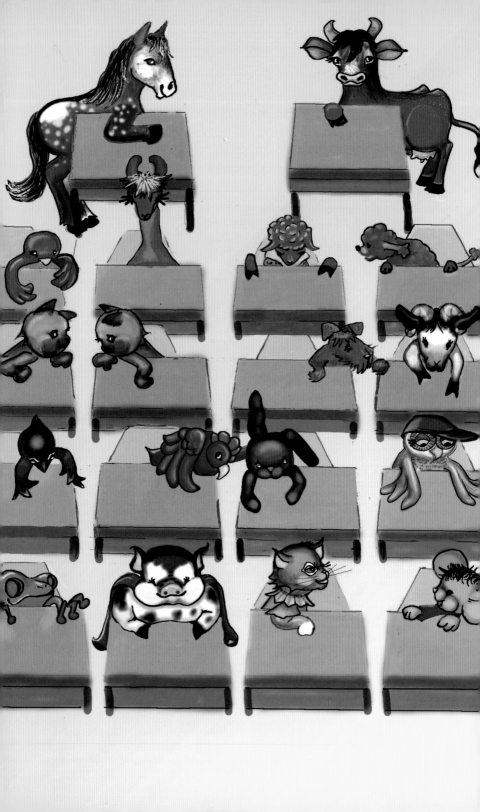

With the Curiosity of a Cat

Chapter One

THE FOUR FRIENDS—PATTY, Freddy, Simon, and Catt—
sat in the front row of Superhero School, waiting for class
to begin. Students filed in, placing the assignments on the
teacher's desk, and staring at the foursome. Everyone had
heard about their adventure last week.

Well, it was mostly Catt's adventure, but they had all
helped her through it.

Catt had been accused of destroying Mouseville, the hidden mouse village outside of town. She had been set up by
Nigel, the diabolical butler, who wanted Catt out of the way,
so he could inherit her family fortune. It was a long ordeal,
but in the end, they had found the proof necessary to right
the wrongs. Nigel went to jail. Catt went home.

And now they were heroes. Everywhere they went, whispers followed and fingers pointed at Patty the pig, Freddy the
frog, Simon the mouse, and Catt the cat. They were renowned
at Superhero School after one week.

Of course, not everyone was happy for them. There were
still some who dubbed them the "Dweeb Squad," claiming
the whole thing was sham. If Mrs. Gristle, the wealthy old

cat widow, hadn't been involved, no one would've taken any notice.

The friends smiled at each other and ignored the recognition—good and bad—from the class.

● ● ●

The air in the classroom crackled with expectation. The lights blinked, the projection screen slid down from the ceiling, and the door shut on its own. Everyone scrambled to find their desks.

"Good morning, students," a voice boomed from the speakers. "Welcome to your second class."

The screen flickered on, revealing the image of an airplane.

"As you know, flying is an important skill necessary for superheroes."

Students looked at one another, uncertain. All but Simon. He'd already spotted the pile of equipment hidden behind the big desk. A small smile curved his mouse lips. Helmets plus backpacks with straps and buckles equaled flying.

"Today, each of you will experience flying, some for the first time."

Simon looked at Catt, who was squirming in her seat, twisting her tail between her paws.

A shrill voice called from the back. "I guess we'll see if pigs really can fly!"

Patty shrunk down in her seat amid the laughter, pulling her purple hood low on her brow. Freddy hopped on top of his desk, but despite his bright green hue, no one saw his tiny scowl. Catt faced the back of the room with Simon on her shoulder, daring anyone to make another taunt. The laughter died immediately.

"If you are finished!" the voice thundered from overhead. "Class will resume in ten minutes at the air field. Collect your equipment and meet your instructors."

The screen rolled up, the lights turned on, and the door swung open.

A penguin, in Superhero School logo jacket, shuffled to the front and passed out helmets and backpacks to every student. A pelican, also in official jacket, handed each student a set of instructions and sent them out the door, staggering under the weight of the packs.

Simon was near the front of the long line when he saw that Catt wasn't beside him.

● ● ●

Catt sunk beneath her desk, hoping no one noticed her. She didn't want to fly! She was a cat. Cats don't fly! She preferred all four paws to remain safely on the ground, thank you very much. But as the line for equipment dwindled, she saw Freddy, Patty, and Simon urging her to join them.

Maybe she could go along and refuse to jump at the last minute. But the very idea of boarding an airplane and flying above the clouds made her stomach drop to her toes. Although she tried to smooth it down, the fur on her tail stood straight up. No way to hide how scared she was from Simon, she'd have to explain.

He'd understand...right?

● ● ●

Simon signaled to Patty and Freddy to go ahead while he returned to Catt. He had his and Catt's equipment already set aside. The penguin instructor and his pelican assistant left for the airfield.

Only Simon and Catt stayed in the classroom.

"Come on, Catt." Simon tried to muster enthusiasm into his voice. He wanted to dance all the way to the plane, but

Catt needed him, and he wouldn't leave without her. He never wanted her to feel alone again.

"Let's grab our gear and get going. We don't wanna miss the plane." When he said plane, Catt ducked back under the desk, her whole body shaking.

"Catt?" Simon approached slowly. "Are you all right?"

She couldn't catch her breath. She didn't want to let anyone down, but she couldn't get on that plane.

"S-S-S-Simon," Catt stuttered and gasped. "I, uh, can't—I can't do this."

Her head spun. All she could see were Simon's wide eyes before everything disappeared.

● ● ●

"CATT!" Simon pulled and poked at his friend. But she didn't wake up. He lifted her eyelid to see her eye roll back in her head.

Catt had been so afraid, she forgot to breathe. Great. How would Simon get them both to the airfield in seven minutes? Especially when one of them was unconscious and ten times his size!

He needed help. Digging through his coat pocket, he wrapped his paw around a whistle. It was for emergencies only, but Simon figured this counted as an emergency.

Pursing his lips, Simon blew with every ounce of air in his lungs, then he listened. Thundering feet sounded from every corner of the building.

Help is on the way. Simon sighed and hoped it would be enough.

=^.,.^=

About Donna Sager Cowan

As the youngest child in a large family, Donna felt lost in the crowd. She entertained herself by making up stories and friends to play with. By age 5, Donna had taught herself to read, and that began her imaginative journey to dreamy castles with princes and fairy godmothers.

Donna is a grandmother, random fact-finder, and encourager. And, yes, she believes she's a superhero.

She lives in California with her family and four cats. (Sadly, no mice like Simon.)

Follow The Superhero School series at
DonnaSagerCowan.com.

Author visits available for your class, school, group, or organization. Scheduling and information at DonnaSagerCowan.com.

Connect on social media at https://linktr.ee/catt.the.cat.

About Diane J. Reid

Diane began illustrating her own stories around age 6. She went on to a 60-plus-year career as an artist, goldsmith, and jeweler, earning multiple degrees in Fine Arts.

Diane took time away from her work to teach art classes at her local elementary schools, and she once crafted a fairy house from driftwood.

She lives along the Central Coast of California—close to the ocean she loves—with her family, three cats, and a dog that might look a bit like one of the Superhero School students.

Follow Diane at instagram.com/dianesdoodledomain/.